D0408779

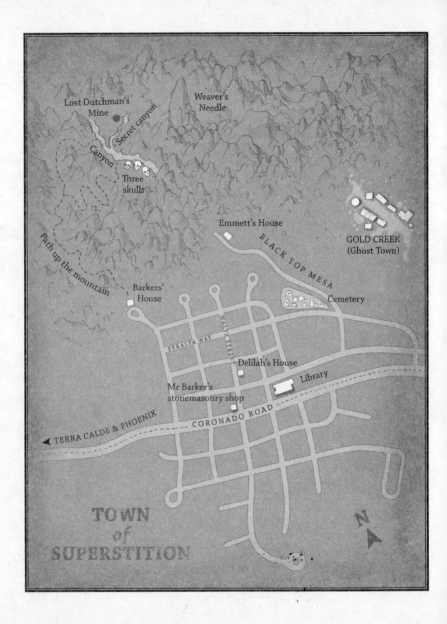

TREASURE ON
SUPERSTITION
MOUNTAIN

BOOK TWO

ELISE BROACH

ILLUSTRATED BY
ANTONIO JAVIER CAPARO

Christy Ottaviano Books

Henry Holt and Company
New York

Henry Holt and Company, LLC
Publishers since 1866
175 Fifth Avenue
New York, New York 10010
mackids.com

Library of Congress Cataloging-in-Publication Data
Broach, Elise.
Treasure on Superstition Mountain / Elise Broach ;
illustrated by Antonio Javier Caparo.—1st ed.
p.   cm.
"Christy Ottaviano books."
Sequel to: Missing on Superstition Mountain.
Summary: Returning to Superstition Mountain, the Barker brothers,
along with their friend Delilah, soon find themselves entangled
in more danger and mystery as they uncover a real treasure.
ISBN 978-0-8050-7763-6 (hardcover)—ISBN 978-0-8050-9640-8 (e-book)
[1. Mountains—Fiction.   2. Brothers—Fiction.   3. Gold mines and mining—Fiction.
4. Superstition Mountains (Ariz.)—Fiction.   5. Arizona—Fiction.
6.   Mystery and detective stories.]   I. Caparo, Antonio Javier, ill.   II. Title.
PZ7.B78083Tr 2012   [Fic]—dc23   2012006475

First Edition—2012 / Designed by Patrick Collins
Printed in the United States of America
by RR Donnelley & Sons Company, Harrisonburg, Virginia

1 3 5 7 9 10 8 6 4 2

For my nephew and niece,
Henry and Anabelle Wheeler

CHAPTER 1
THE SURPRISE IN THE BACKPACK

"CAREFUL! She might hear you."

Henry glanced at his open bedroom door, but there was no sign of their mother lurking in the hallway. He and his brothers were clustered in front of the closet, where Delilah's neon pink backpack had been stowed for two entire weeks, untouched.

How he'd managed to accomplish that still astonished Henry. Simon and Jack were dying to see what he and Delilah had found on Superstition Mountain, and Henry was dying to show it to them. But after the hullabaloo of their adventure—their forbidden trip up the mountain to retrieve the three skulls on the ledge in the canyon; Delilah falling and breaking her leg; Henry staying behind with her while Simon and Jack went for help; finding the ancient saddlebag with the map and pouch of coins, the mysterious gunshot, and Henry's discovery of a small, secret canyon—they had to be extra careful not to arouse the suspicion of their parents. Officially, they were grounded for two weeks . . . which meant there was no escaping Mrs. Barker's watchful eye. Simon pointed out that while it was not a particularly imaginative punishment for flouting the warning to stay off the mountain, it wasn't an unreasonable one either. Henry was just glad their parents hadn't said a month.

Anyway, the timing was good, since Delilah's mother was sufficiently unnerved by Delilah's injury to have whisked her away to her grandparents' condo complex in Tucson, which, according to Delilah, couldn't have been more safe or boring. She and Henry had talked on the phone twice since she left. "Don't show Simon and Jack what we found in the saddlebag," she'd begged. "I want to be there. Can't you wait till I get back?"

So despite the impatient demands of his brothers, Henry had promised to save the backpack's revelations for Delilah's return. And now here it was Monday afternoon. Delilah was home again, off crutches, in a new walking cast, and coming over momentarily. And, hooray! They weren't grounded anymore.

"But can't you just show us the coins?" Jack complained, more softly this time. "You said they're just like the ones Uncle Hank collected in his coin box. Delilah won't care if you do that."

Hank Cormody, for whom Henry was named, had been their father's favorite uncle—a cattle-wrangling, gambling, hard-living former U.S. Cavalry scout with a taste for adventure that Henry longed to find an echo of in himself. The Barkers had inherited his house here in the strange little town of Superstition, Arizona, a few months ago, when Uncle Hank died after a very long and eventful life.

Jack leaned forward on his knees, tugging the backpack out from the closet's morass of shoes, board games, and balls. Jack was six, but he was almost as big as Henry, who was ten, and far bolder. Simon was eleven, full of interesting ideas, and given to concocting schemes and issuing orders. Henry was the imaginative, bookish one. He got along with everybody and liked to use big words (though not always exactly the right way).

"No, Jack," Henry repeated. "I promised Delilah."

Jack groaned and turned to Simon for support, but luckily, since Henry had been the one to carry the backpack down the mountain, even Simon seemed willing to defer to him.

"We can wait," Simon said. "She'll be here any minute."

So they sat on the floor of Henry's room, with the sun streaming through the window and a feeling gathering in the air of something about to happen. The craggy bluffs and peaks of Superstition Mountain huddled ominously right outside.

Just then they heard the doorbell and, a moment later, their mother's voice, welcoming Delilah into the house. "Oh, honey! Look at your leg. How are you doing? Are you getting used to walking with the cast?"

Henry jumped up and ran to the bedroom door. "We're back here!" he called. Delilah appeared, clunking unevenly on her white cast, brown braids slapping her shoulders. Henry, who hadn't seen her since that strange, scary night in the canyon, felt suddenly shy. But Delilah thumped eagerly into the bedroom, grinning at all of them. "Hey," she said.

"Wow!" Jack stared at her cast. "Cool!" He knocked on it with his fist.

"Jack," Simon said, "her leg's broken! Don't pound on it."

"That's okay," Delilah said. "I can't feel anything."

"It doesn't hurt?" Henry asked. He thought of Delilah cringing in pain on the canyon floor, her bruised, cut leg propped awkwardly in front of her.

"Nope," Delilah answered cheerfully. "It's like walking around on a block of wood."

"Like a pirate!" Henry exclaimed. "A peg-leg pirate. Like in *Peter Pan*." Henry remembered books he had read as vividly as if he had lived through them, as if their characters and events had been part of his real life.

"Yeah, like that," Delilah agreed. "Except I can't take it off and bonk people over the head with it."

Jack grabbed a handful of markers from Henry's desk drawer and squatted next to Delilah's cast. "Can we draw on it?"

Henry noticed that, unlike the casts of kids at school, this one wasn't covered in colorful cartoons and flowers and messages. It had a few shaky cursive signatures running across it and one "Get well soon!" That was it.

"Sure," Delilah said. She sat down and propped the cast in front of them. "My grandparents signed it, and some of the old people they play cards with, but they just wrote regular stuff."

Jack eagerly set to work, brandishing a blue marker as if it were a spear. Simon rolled his eyes. "Don't draw something dumb, Jack," he said, but Henry could tell he wanted to write on the cast too.

Delilah held her foot still while Jack printed his name in crooked letters and drew big arrows around it.

"What are the arrows for?" Simon asked.

"They make it look good," Jack replied. "Like my name is FLYING."

Simon smirked and proceeded to sign his name boldly in black. He drew a skull and crossbones next to it.

"Ha!" Delilah said. "Like the skulls in the canyon."

Henry sighed. Why didn't he think of that? Simon always had the best ideas. Henry wrote his name carefully in green, then made a neat paw print for Josie.

Delilah smiled. "Aw . . . Josie. Where is she?"

"Probably outside," Henry said, "hunting something." Josie had managed to catch a ground squirrel last week and had carried its tiny carcass to the back deck in triumph, held gingerly in her mouth the way she transported all her most prized possessions, from squeaky cat toys to the crunched wads of paper she liked to pilfer from the wastebasket. She'd set the dead squirrel proudly in front of the sliding glass doors for all to see. "Ugh!" their father had protested at the time. "That puts me off my dinner." Their mother had calmly scooped it up and

dumped it in the garbage can. "Cats are predators. She's just following her natural instincts," she said. Now, in the early mornings and evenings, they often saw Josie stalking across the yard, clearly hoping for a repeat of her good fortune.

"Okay, okay," Simon said impatiently, gathering the markers and tossing them back into the desk drawer. "Can we finally look in the backpack? I want to see the coins and this map you've been telling us about. We've been waiting forever."

"You really didn't show them?" Delilah asked Henry in surprise.

Henry blinked. "I told you I wouldn't."

"I know, but I figured you were just saying that to make me feel better." Delilah pulled her backpack smugly into her lap. "Good! Now we can all look at them together."

Jack bounced on his knees. "Show us! Show us!"

"Keep it down," Simon warned. "Mom'll come." He quietly closed the bedroom door.

Henry looked at Delilah. "Now?"

She nodded, patting the pockets until she located the one where Henry had placed the map and coin pouch that they'd found two weeks ago in the old leather saddle-bag on the canyon floor.

Carefully, she took out the small brown sack with the coins in it. She cupped it in her palm for a moment, then passed it to Henry. "You do it," she said.

The pouch felt heavy and lumpy in Henry's hand. He untied the rawhide string and tugged open the fragile neck of the sack, sending a shower of dust and leather fragments onto the stretch of carpet between them.

"That looks OLD," Jack commented.

Henry reached in and pinched a coin between his fingers. Its surface was cold to the touch. He drew it from inside the bag.

Simon took it from him and scrutinized it in the sunlight. "Look . . . it *is* the same. Just like the ones from Uncle Hank's coin collection."

"It has the guy with the long hair and the girly ribbon!" Jack crowed. He grabbed the pouch from Henry and turned it upside down, shaking it, "Let's see how many coins there are."

Coin after coin tumbled out, dark with age. They clinked softly against one another as they landed in the middle of the carpet.

"Jack, careful," Henry told him. "They're so old they're . . . *decrepit*." He was just appreciating the sound of that fancy word leaving his mouth when he froze.

"Oh!" Delilah gasped.

There in the jumble of ancient coins was something that didn't look like a coin at all.

Something small and jagged, the size of a berry.

Something that glinted in the sunlight.

Even Jack was completely silent, his eyes huge.

"Hey . . ." Simon picked it up, and Henry thought it almost seemed to glow.

"Is that . . . ?" Delilah whispered.

Henry stared in amazement.

CHAPTER 2
BURIED TREASURE

"IT'S GOLD! IT'S GOLD! We found GOLD!" Jack cried.

"*Shhhhh!*" They all turned on him at once.

"Everything okay?" Mrs. Barker's voice drifted down the hallway.

Simon glared at Jack, scrambled to his feet, and quickly opened the bedroom door. "Yeah, Mom, we're fine. Jack's just being loud."

"Sorry," Jack whispered, chastened.

They waited a minute, in case she was coming, but then they heard the distant rustling in her office and knew she'd returned to work. Mrs. Barker's latest medical illustration project was a book on kidney disease, which meant that her sketchpad was filled with drawings of misshapen kidneys—swollen ones that looked about to burst and tiny shriveled ones that resembled rotting fruit, covered in strange bruises and lesions.

When Simon sat back down, Henry reached out and took the nugget. It was surprisingly heavy. Henry rubbed his thumb across the rough surface, and its glitter blinded him.

"Gold," he repeated, wonder-struck. "So there *is* a gold mine somewhere in that canyon."

Delilah grabbed it and held it aloft. "But where? We didn't see anything that looked like a mine."

"What about the gunshot?" Henry persisted. "Maybe that's why they were shooting at us! Because we were getting too close to the secret gold mine."

"But you said the shot was probably hunters," Simon said. "That's what the police thought too."

Henry lifted his shoulders helplessly. "I don't know what it was." When he thought of the echoing boom of the shot in the canyon—the shock of it—it was hard to believe it had really happened. Even at the time, it seemed like there had to be some other explanation.

"Let me hold it," Jack insisted. "It's my turn." Delilah dropped it into his outstretched palm.

"I wonder how much it's worth!" Simon rubbed his

hands together. "I mean, this has got to be several ounces, don't you think? How much do people pay for an ounce of gold?"

Henry shook his head. "I don't know. We could look it up on the computer . . . but we'll have to wait till Mom's finished."

Their mother was annoyingly fussy about the boys' computer use. It mustn't interfere with her work or their father's accounting for his stonemasonry business. As a principle, she thought their time was much better spent outdoors. Also, she had a constant worry that they would accidentally delete one of her files. But to be fair, the internet was so unreliable in Superstition that they could never count on doing what they wanted on the computer even on the rare occasions when their mother gave them permission to use it.

"We're RICH!" Jack declared, plunking the nugget down in front of them.

"Well, probably not," Simon corrected him. "But if we could ever find that gold mine, we would be. Wait— what about the map? That was the other thing you found in the saddlebag, right? Where is it?"

Delilah delved into the side pocket of the backpack

again. "It's here. But we didn't see anything that looked like the symbol for a gold mine." Gently, she extracted the tattered brown paper and opened it across the carpet.

In the glare of the sun, it looked even older and more frail than it had that day in the canyon, Henry thought. The dark ink marks were faded and hard to decipher.

"The squiggly line is a creek," he explained to Simon and Jack. "We think these spikes are trees, and the up-side down *V*'s are the mountain peaks all around."

"And these," Delilah added, her finger hovering over two jagged parallel lines, "show where the canyons are. This is the canyon with the skulls, and here's the little secret canyon Henry found."

"Hmmm," Simon said, leaning over it. "So nothing that looks like a gold mine?"

Henry shook his head. "I don't see anything. But what kind of symbol would it be, anyway? A black circle? An *X*?" He was thinking of the map in *Treasure Island*, the *X* that marked the spot where the treasure chest was buried.

"I don't know," Simon said. "But you're right. I don't see anything that looks like a gold mine." He sat back on his heels and rubbed one hand over his hair, making it even spikier than usual. "Where can we find out more about gold mines?"

"There was some stuff about the Lost Dutchman's Mine in that book of legends I got at the library," Delilah said. "But it was pretty much what we'd already heard. Jacob Waltz found it, kept the location a secret, and lived off the gold for years until he died. Nobody else ever discovered where the gold mine was."

Henry jumped up and crossed the room to his night-stand, where a stack of books teetered perilously close to his pillow. "There's the chapter about Superstition Mountain in that Arizona history book we checked out," he said, pulling it from the pile. "But it doesn't have much about gold miners." He thumbed through the pages. "Maybe we should go back to the library?"

"With that creepy librarian?" Jack shuddered. "Ugh."

"Oh, come on, Jack," Simon scoffed. "You can't be scared of a librarian. That's goofy. And we have to renew those books anyway."

"I'm not SCARED," Jack argued. "She's weird! And her name was on a tombstone."

That made Henry shudder. He thought of the day in the cemetery, the area of old graves, with JULIA ELENA THOMAS carved across one of the tilted headstones.

"Our name was on a tombstone," Simon reminded him. "Thomas . . . Barker . . . they're common names."

Henry looked at him doubtfully. It was what Simon had said at the time, but it hadn't seemed a good explanation then, and it didn't now.

Simon gathered the coins and dropped them back in the pouch. He cupped the gold nugget in his hand for a minute, rolling it over his palm. "Okay, let's put it back," he said. "Take one last look." He lifted it into a beam of sunlight from Henry's window, where it flashed brilliantly. They all stared.

"What if we found lots of gold rocks just like that?" Jack whispered. "What if we found a HUNDRED?"

"If we find that gold mine, there will be more than a hundred," Simon said, slipping the nugget into the sack with the coins. "That's why we need to go to the library."

CHAPTER 3
THE PHOTOGRAPH

DELILAH SLIPPED THE POUCH and the map carefully into the side pocket of her backpack and slung it over her shoulder.

"Wait!" Simon said. "You can't take that. We need to keep it here."

Delilah frowned. "But it's my backpack."

"We could hide the map and the gold somewhere else," Henry suggested.

Simon shook his head. "If it's in our stuff, Mom might find it. She won't go nosing around in Delilah's backpack. That's the best place for it." He turned to Delilah. "If you take it home, your mom might look through it. You don't need it until school starts, so what difference does it make?"

Delilah balanced uneasily on her cast, still holding

the backpack. "I just don't like leaving it here, is all," she said.

"It'll be safer," Henry told her. "Please?"

She looked at him, thinking. "You guys better not let anything happen to it. Or spill anything on it. Or get it all crumpled and dirty."

Who cares about that? Henry thought. *It's a backpack!* It was meant to get crumpled and dirty; that just meant you were using it for interesting purposes. But Delilah's did have a crisp newish look to it.

She reluctantly handed the backpack to Simon. "Okay."

Simon shoved it far back in Henry's closet, piling the mess of shoes and game boxes in front of it. "There," he said. "Mom won't be digging around in that. Now let's go to the library."

The boys had almost reached the front door when they realized Delilah wasn't with them. She was standing in the hallway, looking forlorn.

"What's the matter with you?" Jack cried. "Hurry up!"

Delilah sighed. "I can't. I can't run. I can't ride my bike. I can't go to the library with you." She bit her lip, looking down at the cast.

"What's all this?" Mrs. Barker appeared in the doorway of her study, pushing her glasses to the bridge of her nose. "Where are you all off to?"

"We were going to go to the library," Simon said. "But Delilah can't come because of her cast." He composed his face in what Henry thought was a very convincing crestfallen expression.

"Well, I could walk," Delilah said. "But it will take me a lot longer than you."

Mrs. Barker squeezed Delilah's shoulder. "That's silly. I don't mind giving you all a ride," she said. "Then if you're up to it, you can walk back, or"—she turned to Simon—"your father can pick you up in a couple of hours, on his way home from work."

Mr. Barker's stonemasonry shop, where he mixed cement and stored slabs of rock for walkways and patios, was right in the center of town, a short distance from the library.

"That would be great!" Simon said jubilantly.

Mrs. Barker pulled the station wagon up to the curb, near the library's sliding doors. "Don't forget to renew anything that might be due," she said.

"Oops, we forgot our books," Henry fretted.

"That's okay, the librarian can renew them automatically. Do you need my library card?"

"They were checked out on mine," Delilah said, "and I brought it." She waved a pink-and-black-striped wallet in the air. "See? My grandparents gave this to me. For breaking my leg. I keep everything in it."

It surprised Henry that anyone would deserve a present for falling down a canyon and breaking her leg, especially since it happened while she was exploring a mountain she'd been expressly forbidden to climb . . . but he had to admit, grandparents were funny that way. They always felt sorry for you and wanted to make things better, even if the problem was entirely your fault. He remembered one time his grandparents had given him a watch for his birthday and he'd accidentally worn it in the shower that very night, ruining it. His parents had been mad at him, but his grandparents bought him another one just like it and mailed it to him the very next day. "Those things happen," his grandma told his mother later. "And Henry was so excited about that watch! He didn't mean to break it. I'm just glad it was something easily replaced."

Jack looked at Delilah's wallet and wrinkled his nose. "Ugh, PINK. Why is everything you own pink?"

"It's not." Delilah tucked the wallet back in her pocket. "But I like pink. It's a happy color."

Simon swung open the car door and reminded Mrs. Barker, "Tell Dad to pick us up, okay? In a couple of hours."

They spilled onto the pavement, which shimmered a hot white in the afternoon sun. It was already over ninety degrees, a baking, steady heat without an ounce of moisture in it.

"I'll tell him to come around four," Mrs. Barker called through the window as she drove away. "Keep an eye on Jack."

Jack's face clouded. "Why does she always say that? I don't need anyone to keep an eye on me."

"Sure you do—" Simon started.

"I do not!" Jack raised his fist.

But Henry interrupted. "It's just because you're the youngest. It doesn't mean anything." And then, to distract him, "Are there any books you want to check out?"

Jack thought for a minute. "I'm going to get a book on snakes," he said sullenly.

"What kind of snakes?" Delilah asked, and Henry shot her a grateful glance.

"Rattlesnakes!" Jack answered as they walked through the doors into the cool sanctum of the library.

Jack glanced around. "Where is she?" he whispered loudly.

"There." Delilah pointed. "Behind the circulation desk." Julia Thomas, the strange black-haired librarian with the nicey-nice voice and the fake smile, was helping an older man in a plaid shirt.

"Shhh," Simon warned. "Let's go back to the local history section. Maybe she won't see us."

They strode quickly across the beige carpet to the low bookshelves marked ARIZONA HISTORY that stood against the wall under a large, bright map of Arizona.

"Look for books about gold mines and miners," Simon said. "Especially anything about the Lost Dutchman's Mine."

The boys crouched in front of the shelves while Delilah bent awkwardly over her cast. They set to work sorting through the thick, tattered volumes.

"Hey!" Jack announced. "Look at this!" He held up a large book with *ARIZONA GOLD!* emblazoned in yellow letters across a black-and-white photograph of two prospectors and a donkey standing in front of a cave. "And it has lots of pictures too."

"That's a good one," Simon said approvingly. "See what's in it."

"Here, I'll help you read the captions," Delilah offered, lowering herself to the floor.

Henry and Simon continued to look through the rows of books. There were so many, on every conceivable topic: pioneers, ranchers, the Apache Indians.

"Here's one," Simon said. *"Mining Towns of the Old West.* There's a section on Arizona. Maybe there will be something about treasure maps in here."

"Ooooh," Henry said suddenly, grabbing the spine of a slim orange book and pulling it from the shelf. *"The Lost Dutchman's Mine."*

He sat next to Simon and began reading about Jacob Waltz, who had come to the Superstitions in the 1870s. Waltz had learned the location of a fabulous gold mine either from the Spanish descendants of Miguel Peralta or from an Apache Indian girl—nobody was certain which—but he would show up in Phoenix year after year with saddlebags full of gold, refusing to tell anyone where the riches had come from. When gold seekers tried to follow him out of town, in the hope of finding the hidden mine, he would lose them in the cliffs and canyons of Superstition Mountain.

Henry read this part aloud to the others. "That's like Uncle Hank," he told them, thinking of the stories about their madcap uncle, winning at poker in one of the little towns surrounding the mountain and then retreating to its crooks and crevices to elude the angry players who chased after him, hoping to reclaim their money.

Henry turned a page to find a photograph of a severe-looking fellow with a bushy beard and a rather garish checked suit.

"Hey," he announced, "here's a picture of Jacob Wal—" Then he stopped.

"What is it?" Delilah asked, scooting closer to him.

"Look at this picture," Henry said softly, his finger falling on the photo next to the picture of Jacob Waltz. It was a faint black-and-white image of a woman. "It looks like—"

"Looks like what?" Simon crawled over to them.

Henry stared at the woman's dark hair, bright eyes, and thin, swooping eyebrows. "It looks like—" he began again.

Jack bounced up and leaned over their shoulders. "It looks like the creepy librarian!"

CHAPTER 4
THE WARNING

SIMON FROWNED. "It does, sort of. But it's such an old photo. It's hard to see what she really looks like."

Delilah sucked in her breath. "Read the caption," she said quietly.

Henry's finger drifted down to the tiny italicized sentence below the photograph. He read aloud, "In his old age, sick with pneumonia and in frail health, Jacob Waltz was cared for by a local woman. . . ." He stared at Delilah and finished helplessly, "Julia Thomas."

"What?" Simon demanded. "Read that again."

"That's her name," Henry said slowly. "Julia Thomas. And it's the same name we saw on the tombstone." He couldn't keep himself from shivering. What did it mean?

"Well," Simon said, pausing, "I guess the woman

who took care of Jacob Waltz all those years ago could be buried in that old part of the cemetery. That's possible."

"But she looks the SAME as the librarian!" Jack protested. "And she lived a hundred years ago! Does that mean the librarian is a GHOST?"

"What's that about ghosts?" A chillingly familiar voice interrupted them, and they looked up to see Mrs. Thomas walking toward them.

How much had she heard? Henry slammed the book shut and pressed it against his chest. Simon quickly swept the other volumes into a stack.

"Hello, children, how are you?" Mrs. Thomas greeted them, her smile pasted on her face in that unsettling way that never reached her eyes. "I'm glad to see all of you back in the library." Her gaze darted over the books at their feet. "Can I help you with something?"

Before she could get any closer, Delilah hauled herself to her feet. "Could you help me get a book from the top shelf?" she asked smoothly. "I can't reach it on account of my cast."

Mrs. Thomas turned to her. "Which one?" she asked as Delilah hobbled away from the stack of books on the floor.

"Up there." Delilah pointed. "The blue one with the gold letters."

Mrs. Thomas reached up and drew a fat book from the top shelf, putting it in Delilah's outstretched hands. "I heard about your little adventure on the mountain," she said.

"You did?" Jack blurted.

"Yes, I did. What a shame Delilah broke her leg."

She started toward their pile of reading material, but Delilah blocked her. "Hey, would you sign my cast?" she asked, lifting it awkwardly in the air.

Mrs. Thomas backed away in distaste.

"Please?" Delilah persisted. "I have a pen."

"Oh, all right." The librarian leaned over Delilah's cast, lips pursed. Quickly, in tightly looped, slanting cursive, she signed her name. Henry noted the absence of any greeting or encouraging remark.

"Thanks," Delilah murmured in defeat as Mrs. Thomas pushed past her to their stack of books.

"Are you looking for ghost stories?" she asked.

"Jack was," Simon volunteered.

Jack glowered at him. "No, I want a book on snakes—" he started, but Delilah and Henry hushed him.

"We don't really have anything like that in this section. But there are some good children's mysteries with a supernatural element. Jack, why don't I take you over to juvenile fiction, and we'll see if we can find you something?" She turned to him expectantly, but he sat rigid, as if nailed to the carpet.

"Oh, that's okay," Delilah interjected. "I can take him over there later. We wanted to check out some more books about Superstition Mountain."

Mrs. Thomas crossed her arms and studied them. "I see that you've chosen some books about mining towns."

Simon shrugged. "We're just looking for anything on the history of this place," he said vaguely.

"Is that all?" For the first time, the strange frozen smile completely left Mrs. Thomas's face. Henry shifted uncomfortably under her unrelenting stare. He saw that her bony fingers were gripping her arms so hard that her knuckles had turned white.

"Well," she said, her words dropping like cold, hard pebbles from her mouth, "the history of this place is not a game for children." She looked at each of them in turn. "The history of this place could get you into trouble."

Simon started to say something in response, but Mrs. Thomas raised her hand and the words died on his tongue.

"What happened to you on the mountain is just the beginning," she said. With that, she turned and walked away.

CHAPTER 5
GOLD CREEK

"Ugh!" JACK SHUDDERED as soon as the librarian was out of earshot. "She is so weird. I bet she IS a ghost."

"There are no such things as ghosts, Jack," Simon said impatiently. "But she is strange. She always seems like she's trying to scare us."

"Well, it's working!" Henry said. "How do you think she knew what happened to us up on the mountain? Who would she be talking to about that?"

"It could only be the policemen, right?" Delilah said thoughtfully. "Unless your parents said something. My mom and I have been out of town."

"Our parents didn't say anything!" Jack protested. "They are not blabbermouths."

Henry considered this. He secretly felt that their mother *was* sort of a blabbermouth. She had a tendency to matter-of-factly reveal things about the boys that she found interesting or touching, but that struck them as deeply embarrassing. Their father, on the other hand, could be counted on to keep anything they told him confidential, but as their mother remarked, that was mostly because he wasn't paying close attention in the first place.

"I didn't say they were," Delilah answered calmly. "Superstition is such a small town. My mom says one of the bad things about small towns is that everybody knows everybody else's business. Maybe that's how she found out." She paused. "What do you think she meant, 'just the beginning'? The beginning of what?"

Even Simon had no answer to that. They looked at each other apprehensively. Henry opened his book across the floor and returned to the page with the photograph of the dark-haired woman, her bright, beady eyes gazing straight ahead. A chill of foreboding washed through him. "It really does look like her," he said weakly. "And she's got the same name!"

Delilah twisted her braid. "Maybe they're related," she suggested. "Maybe the Julia Thomas in the picture is the other one's great-great-great-grandmother."

"That's possible," Simon said. "Or they could just have the same name." He studied the stack of books in front of him. "If we check these out, she'll know too much about what we're doing."

"Yeah," Henry agreed. "The covers are so *conspicuous*." He glanced down at his book with *The Lost Dutchman's Mine* in large letters across it. The title would give away everything. Mrs. Thomas would quickly figure out that they were interested in the gold mine.

"We'd better leave that one here," Simon decided. "Read as much as you can right now, Henry. I'll look up which mining towns were in this area. Delilah, can you take Jack over to the kids' section to find a book on ghosts? That way we'll at least have something to check out."

"Sure," Delilah said, standing up. "Come on, Jack."

"But I don't want a book about ghosts," Jack complained. "I want a book on SNAKES. And I want to find out stuff about the gold mine."

"We'll find out about the gold mine later," Delilah told him. "Right now we need something to keep that librarian from figuring out what we're really doing."

Henry thought for a minute. "A *decoy*."

"What's that?" Jack asked.

"A book we can check out that will throw her off the scent," Henry explained. "Like a book on ghosts . . . or snakes."

"That's just as important as finding out about the gold mine," Delilah added. Mollified, Jack scrambled to his feet and followed her to the children's area.

Henry flopped on his stomach with his chin in his hands and went back to reading about Jacob Waltz and his secret gold mine.

"Hey," he told Simon, "it says here that Jacob Waltz's house was destroyed in a flood. That's how he got sick with pneumonia and ended up moving in with Julia Thomas so she could take care of him. But people later found $15,000 in gold under his bed!"

Simon raised his eyebrows. "That's a lot! Back then, it would have been a fortune."

"The book says it was high-quality gold ore . . . and everyone wondered where it had come from. They hadn't seen anything like that from Superstition Mountain before." Henry kept reading. "Hey, listen to this: the rumor was, he left behind a map to the mine! With Julia Thomas. And for a while after his death, she tried to find the mine, and then when she couldn't, she made a living selling the directions to people."

Simon looked impressed. It occurred to Henry that this was exactly the kind of scheme Simon himself would have pursued.

"Did anyone ever find it?"

Henry continued reading to himself. He shook his head. "Nope, nobody ever found it."

"So there ARE treasure maps to the gold mine?" Simon cried excitedly. He rubbed his hands together. "That's what we have to look for! Maybe the map you and Delilah brought back from the mountain is one of them."

Henry thought of the dark tattered paper with its crude drawings. Nothing on it had resembled the symbol for a gold mine. But why bother to draw a map unless you were showing someone how to get to somewhere important? To uncover the map's secrets, they would have to think like Uncle Hank . . . the way a real explorer would.

Simon sat up suddenly and pushed his book toward Henry. "Hey, Hen, look at this. It's a map of the Phoenix area around 1880, showing the locations of the old mining towns. When did Jacob Waltz live here?"

Henry glanced down at the printed columns under the picture of the austere man with the beard. "He came to this area in the 1870s and died in 1891."

"So this would be about right. And look . . . here's Superstition, and there's a mining town right here. Gold Creek."

"Do you think it's still there?" Henry asked.

Simon shook his head. "It's just outside of town, and I haven't heard of it, have you? It says here that most of the mining towns closed down in the early 1900s, when the gold ran out." He paused, reading silently for a moment, then looked at Henry. "Listen to this—they became ghost towns."

"Ghost towns! Maybe that's the ghost town the policeman was talking about," Henry said. "The one we're not supposed to explore because it's too dangerous."

Simon's eyes brightened, and his mouth pursed in a calculating way that Henry knew all too well. He had the sudden certain feeling that they would soon be exploring a ghost town.

CHAPTER 6
AN UNEXPECTED VISITOR

HENRY DIDN'T EVEN KNOW what a ghost town looked like. "Do you think it's just a bunch of old buildings, or what?" he asked Simon.

"I guess," Simon said. "There are pictures here, but none of Gold Creek." He turned his book toward Henry. Together they scanned the dim photos of run-down storefronts and buildings with collapsing roofs.

"It looks like they could fall down right on top of you," Henry said.

"Yeah," Simon agreed. "We'll have to be really careful."

At that moment, Jack came charging up with a thin orange book clutched in one hand. "Look what I got!" he yelled. "*In a Dark, Dark Room.* It's all ghost stories, and I can read some of them myself."

"I remember that book," Henry said fondly. "It has this story about a girl who always wears a green ribbon around her neck—"

"Don't spoil it," Delilah interrupted. "That's the best story." Delilah was carrying a book with a photo of a rattlesnake on the cover and the rather alarming title *Rattle of DEATH!*

"And this one!" Jack said, snatching it from her. "A book on rattlesnakes with lots of pictures."

"Cool," Henry said. "You can learn all about them."

"So what did you find out?" Delilah asked.

Henry and Simon quickly recounted their discoveries about Jacob Waltz's treasure map and the abandoned mining town of Gold Creek.

"Do you think it's the ghost town?" Jack exclaimed. "The one we're not supposed to go to?" He turned to Delilah. "It doesn't have real ghosts in it," he explained condescendingly. "They just call it that."

Delilah rolled her eyes. "Yeah, I know," she said. "We talked about that place before."

Simon began reshelving the pile of books, checking the labels on their spines to slot them in the correct place. "Gold Creek is so close to Superstition, it has to be the same town," he said. "We can get there on our bikes."

Henry swallowed. "Do you think it's safe? The buildings in those pictures look like they're falling apart."

"Cool!" Jack cried.

"Yeah," Simon said. "It's like a ruin. Who knows what we'll find there."

Delilah touched her cast. "I can't ride anywhere," she said, dejected. "I hate this!"

Henry felt a small twinge of envy. He briefly wished *he* had such an easy excuse for not taking part in Simon's harebrained schemes.

Jack rapped the plaster with his knuckles. "Yep, you can't come," he said, not unsympathetically. "I sure am glad I didn't break MY leg."

"You guys could wait to go to the ghost town until I get my cast off," Delilah suggested. "It's only a couple more weeks."

Simon snorted. "Why would we do that?"

Delilah's eyes flashed. "Because I would wait for you!" she snapped, then lowered her voice. "And . . ." Henry could tell she was struggling to think of a compelling argument. Finally, she tossed her braid in defiance. "The gold and the map are in *my* backpack. I could have taken it home with me, but I didn't."

This struck Henry as quite circumstantial—they could have put the gold and the map anywhere.

"We could have put those anywhere," Simon scoffed. "We just decided to leave them in your backpack."

"So your mom wouldn't find them!" Delilah straightened her shoulders and said disapprovingly, "You're using me."

Henry looked from Delilah to Simon. "Maybe we don't all have to go," he suggested. "I could stay with Delilah."

Delilah's face softened, and she sent him a grateful glance—so grateful that Henry felt instantly guilty. It was horrible to get credit for being kind when your intentions were really cowardly or self-serving.

"Don't be silly, Hen," Simon said. "We need you. Don't you want to explore a ghost town? Think of all the cool stuff we might find."

Henry bit his lip. He *did* want to go exploring. He remembered the thrill of finding the secret canyon, the excitement of discovering a place nobody else knew about. He'd felt like Uncle Hank, boldly venturing where nobody else would dare to. The ghost town would be like that too; the sense of danger was what made it interesting, what made it worth exploring. If he was ever truly going to be like Uncle Hank, Henry realized, this is what it would take. You couldn't change your personality, but you could change your *choices*. You could consciously choose adventure over playing it safe.

Surprisingly, Delilah seemed to have relented. "You should go," she said to Henry. "You found the saddlebag in the canyon. You're good at noticing things."

And then Henry felt a flicker of pride, the way you do when someone gives you a small, specific compliment that you know in your heart to be true.

Delilah said resignedly, "You'll just have to go to the ghost town without me. When you come back, tell me everything about it, okay?"

"Okay," Henry agreed.

"Hey, guys!" Mr. Barker's cheerful voice carried through the quiet of the library. "Ready to go?" He walked toward them from the circulation desk, where Mrs. Thomas was watching him intently.

Quickly, they all got to their feet, leaving the Arizona history section just as they'd found it, with the books neatly back on the shelves and no visible sign of their research.

"We just have to check out a couple of books for Jack," Simon told their father, and Delilah showed the covers.

"Ewww . . . snakes!" Mr. Barker said, recoiling. "And ghosts, huh? Pretty exciting stuff. Nothing for the rest of you? I can wait if you want to browse some more. Hey, Delilah—look at that cast!"

He crouched on the carpet and knocked on it with his knuckles, and Henry thought, not for the first time, that Mr. Barker and Jack were a lot alike. "Whoa! That's about as hard as the cement I poured today." He grinned up at her. "Can I sign it?"

"Sure," Delilah said, a little shyly.

Simon groaned. "Dad, don't be weird," he ordered. "She doesn't want you to sign it."

"Why not?" Mr. Barker asked, perplexed. "It's good to have it covered with signatures. Makes you look popular."

"It's okay," Delilah said. "I don't care if he signs it." She obligingly stuck out her foot, and Mr. Barker took a pen from his shirt pocket and scribbled his name with a flourish. Above it, he wrote, "Break a leg, kiddo!" and winked at Delilah. "That's what they say in the theater to wish the actors good luck in a play."

"Really? How come?" Delilah asked.

Mr. Barker shrugged. "No idea. But the boys can ask their aunt Kathy for an answer. She's done a lot of theater, and she's coming for a visit on Thursday."

"She is?" All three boys spun to face their father.

Their aunt Kathy was their mother's younger sister, funny and chatty and thoroughly indulgent of her three nephews, since she was still single and had no children of her own.

"Yep. Last-minute plans for your mother and me to go away for our anniversary. I just heard about it myself."

"She's going to STAY with us?" Jack asked, bouncing on his toes. "Without you there?"

That was intriguing, Henry had to admit, because as often as Aunt Kathy had visited, and even babysat for the occasional Saturday evening, Mrs. Barker had never actually trusted her to watch the boys overnight. "I adore your aunt Kathy, but she doesn't always have the best judgment. She hasn't been around children that much. Sometimes she doesn't know what's appropriate," their mother had explained when the boys once asked why this was. Of course the lack of good judgment and ignorance about what was appropriate were exactly the things that made Aunt Kathy so much fun.

"Yes, she's staying with you. Your mother has decided you're finally old enough. Or Aunt Kathy is," he added thoughtfully.

"That'll be great," Simon said.

"I can't wait to see her," Henry added.

"Yeah!" Jack shouted, and raced toward the door of the library.

"Wait, Jack," Delilah called after him. "We have to check out your books."

But Jack burst through the doors without even slowing down.

"Stay out of the parking lot, buddy," Mr. Barker cautioned him.

Mrs. Thomas waited for them at the circulation desk, her eerie smile fixed on Mr. Barker. "Hello, there," she said in her syrupy way. "You must be Simon, Henry, and Jack's father. I can see the family resemblance."

"That I am," Mr. Barker said, extending his hand. "Jim Barker. I hope I don't look too much like these goofballs."

"I'm Julia Thomas," the librarian replied, and Henry and Delilah exchanged a quick glance. She paused. "I heard about your children's mishap up on the mountain."

"You did?" Mr. Barker looked surprised. "How did you hear about that?"

Mrs. Thomas seemed slightly taken aback, and Henry realized that, like Jack, Mr. Barker could be quite useful with his bluntness. "Well, I . . . I saw Officer Myers the other night at a meeting," she said. "And he told me."

Now, why would she be going to a meeting with Officer Myers? Henry wondered.

"Oh," Mr. Barker said easily. "Officer Myers was a

big help to us." He ruffled Henry's curls. "I wish I could hire him full-time to keep track of my boys."

The thought of stern, broad-faced Officer Myers tailing them around all day made Henry cringe.

Mrs. Thomas studied Mr. Barker with her tight smile. "I'm sure you do! They seem prone to mischief, these three." She glanced at Delilah. "Four."

While she said this nicely enough, Henry thought there was an edge to her voice. Their father seemed to sense it too, because he abruptly appeared to have had enough of the conversation.

He gestured to Delilah, who was clutching the books and watching their exchange with wide eyes. "Well, we just need to check these out and then we'll be on our way," he said.

Delilah put *In a Dark, Dark Room* and *Rattle of DEATH!* on the counter and unzipped her new pink-and-black wallet to find her library card. "We need to renew the books we checked out last time," she added.

Mrs. Thomas grunted dismissively, tapped the computer keyboard, then scanned the books' barcodes. She pushed them across the counter. "It was nice to meet you," she said to Mr. Barker. "I do hope you and your wife will keep a closer eye on your sons. I told them the mountain is far too dangerous a place for children."

"Oh, we know that," Mr. Barker said curtly. "Maybe you can convince them to start *reading* about adventures instead of having them. Have a good day."

He turned and led the way out of the library, with Simon, Henry, and Delilah fast on his heels. Jack was poking a stick in the dirt of a flower bed next to the building.

The doors had barely closed behind them when Mr. Barker said, "She is certainly annoying. And librarians are usually so pleasant."

That was true, Henry thought. The librarian at the big public library in their old town in Illinois had been warm and welcoming, always eager to suggest books they would like, interested in their stories about school or about Josie.

"Ugh," Jack said. "She is a tricky one, always SPYING on us. Where's my snake book?" He grabbed it from Delilah.

"Well, I'm not sure what her problem is," Mr. Barker said. "But you guys had better try to stay out of trouble at the library. She doesn't seem like she'd be very understanding." He paused. "And she's right about the mountain. You know that."

"Yes, Dad, we do," Simon said, beleaguered. "And you know the reason we went back up the mountain, which even *Mom* said was the right thing to do."

That was a bit of a stretch, Henry thought. Their mother had said the only reason she wasn't *more upset* with them was that she knew they were trying to do the right thing by bringing back the three skulls they'd found on the ledge, so that they could be identified. She never said it was the right thing to go up the mountain.

Mr. Barker seemed about to point out this flaw in Simon's logic himself, so Henry interrupted him. "Hey, Dad . . . did the coroner ever figure out anything more about how those Texas boys died?" He pictured that day in the canyon when they first saw the three gleaming white skulls, and shivered. Who could have known all that would come after?

Mr. Barker shook his head grimly. "I think I told you what we heard. The one boy must have fallen and cracked his skull. The coroner's office suspects there were other injuries as well, but because they don't have the skeletons, there's no way of knowing. The theory is, the other boys stayed with him, and they all died of dehydration. Could happen to anyone in a place like that . . . which is why you need to stay off the mountain."

"We know, Dad," the boys chorused.

"And you too, Delilah," Mr. Barker added, tugging her long braid. "These knuckleheads came back unscathed. You're the one with a broken leg. Don't let them talk you into any more of their exploits."

Delilah smiled at him but said nothing, following Henry into the car for the ride home.

CHAPTER 7
ANOTHER EXPEDITION

THE NEXT DAY, after breakfast had been eaten, beds made, and Josie fed her coveted mix of kibbles and tuna fish, Simon delicately approached their mother with the proposition that the boys go for a bike ride. Secretly, the night before, he had mapped out the route to the ghost town and determined that it was only a fifteen- or twenty-minute ride from their house.

"We're going for a bike ride on that road by the cemetery today," Simon said as Mrs. Barker loaded the dishwasher. "Is that okay?"

"Which road by the cemetery?" Mrs. Barker looked at them sharply. "Not the highway?"

"No!" Simon said. "I know we're not allowed on the highway. That little curvy road. There isn't a lot of traffic there."

Mrs. Barker said nothing, wiping her hands on a dish towel.

"Please, Mom," Simon continued. "We've been grounded for two weeks! We didn't get to ride our bikes anywhere."

"And why was that?" Mrs. Barker asked coolly.

"I'm not saying it wasn't our fault," Simon replied, his voice even. "I'm just saying we're . . ."

"*Stir-crazy,*" Henry interjected. He reached under the table and stroked Josie, who was weaving between his legs, the tip of her black tail twitching.

Mrs. Barker smiled a little. "I don't know," she said. "I need to think about it."

"Josie!" Jack called from down the hallway.

Josie twitched her ears and stared at the doorway in a mixture of irritation and curiosity.

"Josie, come here!" Skeptically, she trotted into the hall.

"Please, Mom," Simon continued. "You probably won't want us riding all over the place when Aunt Kathy's here."

"You are certainly right about that," Mrs. Barker said. "Aunt Kathy is going to have her hands full as it is."

"So is it okay? For us to go today?"

"I told you, I need to think about it."

Simon groaned. "Well, how long is that going to take?"

"Simon," Mrs. Barker warned.

"That's all right. We can play in the yard for a while," Henry said quickly. He knew from long experience that if they pressured their mom to make a decision too quickly, the answer was more likely to be no. "Come on, Simon," he said. "We can play *Titanic* again." They had started a game on the deck a few days ago that involved hanging on to the railing of their sinking ship and jumping onto life rafts below, which were really crushed cardboard moving boxes strewn around the yard. The best part was fighting each other for space on the rafts.

"Jack," they both yelled.

"What?" Jack demanded. He came pounding down the hall with Josie clutched to his chest, wrapped inside one of their mother's reusable green net shopping bags.

"Jack! Is that one of my bags?" Mrs. Barker demanded. "And what are you doing to poor Josie?"

"We're playing," Jack said evasively.

"Honey, what are you playing? Look at her! She doesn't like that."

Indeed, Josie's ears were pressed flat against her skull, and her claws were poking angrily through the netting. She glared at them balefully.

"We're playing panther," Jack said, unfazed. "I'm the hunter, and I just trapped her in my net. Now I'm taking her back to my hunter camp to skin her."

Henry tried not to imagine what "skinning" was going to involve.

"That is not a good game for a cat," Mrs. Barker told him. "Here, give her to me," she ordered, disentangling Josie from the netting over Jack's loud protests. "You boys clearly need to get outside. I guess you can go for that bike ride. Be sure you put on sun lotion. You'll be home for lunch?"

Simon shot Henry a secret look of triumph. "Sure, Mom. We might go to Delilah's, but we'll call from there and tell you," he promised.

"Okay. Don't forget."

Josie darted from the room in disgust, and a few minutes later, the boys, well slathered in lotion, were pedaling down Peralta Way toward the cemetery. When they crossed Waltz Street, where Delilah lived, Henry felt a little guilty. He knew how much she wished she could come with them. But at least they'd promised to go directly to her house after the ghost town so they could tell her all about it.

"What do you think we should be looking for?" Henry asked Simon as they rode past the dusty, rain-starved yards and the flamboyant cactuses, with their long spines.

"More *gold*," Simon said. "But I doubt we'll find any. Mining equipment? A map would be good. Anything that might have information about the Lost Dutchman's Mine."

They passed the cemetery, with its ornate wrought-iron gates and its stark rows of white headstones. Henry squinted down the long corridors, looking for the section with the older tombstones. When he couldn't see it, he felt vaguely relieved.

"You really think there's GOLD there?" Jack asked before he sucked in a deep breath and held it as they rode by the cemetery.

"Well, there could be," Simon said, "but it seems unlikely. Emmett told us the historical society was filled with people looking for gold, remember? Wouldn't a mining town so close to the mountain be the first place they'd explore?"

"Hey, isn't this Emmett's road?" Henry asked. Now they were crossing a narrow gravel lane, full of ruts.

Simon nodded. "I think so. Look at the sign—Black Top Mesa. That's it."

Henry glanced to the left, where Superstition Mountain huddled darkly, like an animal waiting to pounce. The dirt road curled beneath it, flanked by a scattering of houses. Emmett Trask's was at the very end, out of sight. Henry thought back to their trip there in search of *Missing on Superstition Mountain*, the historical society booklet with its list of the unexplained disappearances and murders on the mountain during the last century—the list that included the three Texas boys whose skulls they'd found. Emmett, a geologist and the former president of the Superstition Historical Society, had gladly offered them a copy of the booklet, but he clearly had nothing but scorn for the way the historical society's current members had become fixated on—what had he called it?—ghost hunting and treasure seeking. That was when the boys and Delilah had discovered that the historical society's current president was none other than the librarian Julia Thomas.

"Wow, there's *nothing* out here," Jack crowed. Clouds of yellow-brown dust rose behind him, so that his bike all but disappeared. On either side of the road were empty fields, rocky ground with brash thatches of grass and the occasional saguaro cactus rising with odd stateliness from the desert underbrush.

"How much farther?" Henry asked Simon, wiping his sweaty face on his sleeve.

Simon peered at the road ahead. "I don't know. It

didn't look far on the map." Suddenly, he slowed down. "Hey, Jack!" he called. "Wait up!"

As Jack braked to a halt in a fog of dust, Simon pointed across the field on their left. "See that, Henry? I bet that's it."

Far from the road, Henry could just make out a jumble of buildings . . . slanting roofs, wood siding, a dilapidated water tower rising among them.

"But that's not on the road," Henry said. "It looks pretty far away. Can we even ride there?"

Jack pedaled back to them, blithely bumping over the dips and ruts. "What's the matter? Why are we stopping?"

"I think we're going to have to turn to the left," Simon told him. "Toward those buildings over there. Start looking for a road—or maybe just a path. This side, okay, Jack?"

"Okay," Jack said agreeably. He raced ahead again.

Simon and Henry followed him, going more slowly now. They watched the roadside for breaks in the terrain or any evidence of a trail heading in the direction of the buildings.

"Here!" Jack yelled, screeching to a stop. "There's a path here. Is this it?"

Simon and Henry caught up to him. There was indeed

an opening in the brush, where the shrubs and grasses gave way to a wide, rutted path. It led in the direction of the ruined buildings.

"That must be it," Simon said. "Let's go!"

They steered off the main road and pedaled over the bumpy ground. Ahead of them, the ghost town waited, dark and quiet in the morning sunlight.

CHAPTER 8
GHOST TOWN

"Wow! Cool!" Jack reached the cluster of falling-down buildings first. He dropped his bike in the dirt and charged up the slatted steps to a sagging porch.

"Jack," Simon warned. "That wood is all rotted. Wait for us."

Henry carefully leaned his bike against the side of the first building. He glanced around. He could see that they were standing in the remnants of a street, with three or four decaying buildings lining either side. These were connected by long wooden porches that formed a kind of sidewalk. Signs hung overhead, but the letters had faded or washed away. The structures were built out of wood so old and weathered that it was in various stages of collapse; roofs sagged, porches had sunk to the ground. Whole planks of siding had fallen off, exposing dark interiors.

One of the buildings had a triangular front and a narrow steeple. Henry realized it must have been a church. At the end of the street, the old wooden water tower rose, like a giant barrel propped on stilts. The place was eerily silent.

"We should stick together," he said apprehensively.

"Yeah," Simon agreed. "Watch out for that broken glass, Jack."

Jack was waiting for them on a porch that was covered with shards of glass. All along the street, windowpanes were broken, leaving sharp teeth of glass or empty squares that framed the black interiors of the stores and offices. Where the glass remained, it was so clouded with dust you couldn't see through it.

"Hey," Jack said, "look at the giant wheel!"

A wagon wheel that was easily five feet in diameter leaned against the corner of the building, with a frayed length of rope coiled at its base. The wheel had sunk partway into the ground, and a tangle of vines grew over it. When Henry looked up the street, he saw tufts of grass growing through floorboards, branches shooting through doorways like grasping fingers. It almost seemed as if the land were steadily reclaiming what had once belonged to it.

"Let's see if we can figure out what the different buildings are," Simon suggested. He stepped carefully onto the porch with Jack and peered through one of the broken panes. "This one must have been a store."

Hesitantly, Henry joined him. The flooring of the porch tilted precariously and creaked underfoot. He immediately pictured it falling apart beneath them and the roof burying them alive. He wondered if true explorers worried like this or if the dangers of what they were doing didn't even occur to them. And did it mean you were more brave if you did worry or if you stayed oblivious?

Through the window was a large room lined with shelves. It had a counter running the length of one side. A chair with a broken leg rested against the rear wall.

"What kind of store was this?" Jack wanted to know, squeezing next to them.

Simon shrugged. "Maybe a grocery store?" He thought for a minute. "Or probably, like, a general store that sold everything. Let's look around."

The wood door was warped and slightly ajar. Gingerly, Simon pushed it. It swung loosely on its hinges. He tapped the floorboards with his foot. "Step exactly where I do. In case some of these are rotten."

Henry and Jack obediently trailed behind him, stepping lightly on the splintered wood. Soon they were standing in the middle of the large, dark room. The only light was confined to two angled squares below the front windows.

The air was hazy with dust. The shelves surrounding them were empty.

"I don't like this place," Henry said. The quiet was unnerving. It would be an excellent place for ghosts, he thought. Any sound would be so out of place it would almost *have* to have a supernatural cause. "It's so . . . *disheveled*."

"Does that mean that there's nothing on the shelves?" Jack asked.

"No," Henry said. "It means that nobody's been taking care of it."

Simon shrugged. "It's just an abandoned building."

"I know," Henry said. "That's what I don't like. Look . . . there's nothing left behind."

"Yep," Jack declared. "They took everything with them."

Henry pictured the people who must have lived in this town so many, many years ago, with their bonnets and floppy hats, beards and petticoats and suspenders. He imagined them bustling into this general store for their weekly shopping, reaching up to the high shelves, collecting goods to fill their wagons. At first, in his mind, they seemed serious and purposeful, fussy in their old-fashioned ways. But really, he decided, they were probably no different from anybody going to the store . . . chatting with their neighbors, bemoaning the price of sugar or beans.

"Maybe there's something behind the counter," Simon said. He crossed the room to the large counter where the cash register would have been. There were shelves behind it and drawers and cupboards below. Simon started opening them one by one. When Henry walked up behind him, he saw that they too were completely bare.

"Let's go to the next one," Jack said impatiently. "There's not any gold here." He turned and ran out of the store, thumping across the sagging porch and jumping to the ground.

"Jack!" Simon yelled. "What did I tell you? You have to be careful."

"I was!" Jack protested, already halfway down the street.

"Jack's right," Henry said to Simon as they emerged into the hot sun. "I don't think we're going to find anything about the gold mine here. It looks like this place was cleared out a long time ago."

Simon sighed. "I know. But it's still worth having a look around."

They wandered along the street. Next to the store was a building that appeared to be the post office, with a grid of wooden cubbies lining the back wall. Simon started to go in, but stopped when he saw that its floor had a gaping black hole in the center. "Whoa," he said, backing up.

"There's nothing in the cubbies anyway," Henry told him, glancing around uneasily. In the field behind the buildings, he could see the strange shapes of old farm equipment—a rusted plow, a wagon turned on its side.

The church was next, with its empty rows of pews. Henry and Simon walked quietly up the center aisle, but nobody had left behind so much as a hymnal.

"Let's go in here," Jack called from across the street. He was standing in front of a three-story building with a squared-off false front. Rows of windows marked the upper floors, and the panes were mostly intact. A large, faded sign hung over the porch, almost bleached to illegibility by the sun. There was a shadowy silhouette of a cat on one side, and Henry could just make out the words "Black Cat Hotel and Saloon."

Henry turned to Simon. "Look," he said. "Like Josie."

"It's the biggest building here," Simon answered. "We should check it out."

They walked over to join Jack, who had climbed the

wide stairs and was standing in the front doorway, peering inside.

"I think it's a hotel!" he told them excitedly. "Some of the keys are still here!"

Henry saw a high counter at the back of the main room and a rack of small hooks behind it. Rusty skeleton keys dangled from some of them. There was a narrow staircase in one corner of the room, but the bottom stairs had rotted away.

"Hey, I think you're right," Simon exclaimed.

They crossed the room to the counter, and Henry stepped behind it. One side had a column of long, flat drawers, many of them missing the handles. He knelt on the sagging floor and began at the bottom, pulling them out one by one. The wood had warped enough to make them stick. Even tugging hard, Henry could sometimes only get a drawer to open partway, though that was enough to see that it was empty.

He shook his head at Simon and Jack. "I don't think there's anything here." He pulled at the top drawer. It rattled but didn't budge. "And this one won't open at all."

Simon leaned over the counter. "That's 'cuz it's locked," he said.

Henry saw that he was right—there was a small metal keyhole in the center of it.

"Why is it locked?" Jack asked excitedly. "Do you think there's GOLD in it?" He bounced on the floor, which creaked ominously.

"Take it easy, Jack," Simon warned.

"Well, if it's locked, there must be something good in there," Jack reasoned. "Even if there's no gold, there could be MONEY." He handed Henry a brown key from the back wall. "Try one of the keys."

Henry shook his head. "That's a room key. It's too big."

"Do you see any other keys back there?" Simon asked. "Maybe on the shelf?" Again, Henry shook his head. "Nope, nothing. And why would someone bother to lock it and put the key so close by?" He grabbed the knob and pulled again, harder this time. The drawer stayed shut.

"Maybe we can use something to pry it open," Simon said thoughtfully. "There's a little gap when you pull on it. Try sticking that key Jack gave you in the gap, and then press down on it. Maybe you can wedge the drawer open."

That struck Henry as a remarkably good idea, and he marveled all over again at Simon's science-y brain, which could always be counted on to figure out a creative use for whatever was on hand.

"Yeah," Jack echoed. "Try that."

"Okay," Henry said, pulling the drawer as hard as he could. He slipped the end of the rusty key into the narrow space between the rim of the drawer and the framing, directly above the lock. Then he pushed down on the top of the key with all his might. The wood splintered immediately, and the drawer jolted open.

"What's there? What's inside?" Jack clamored.

Henry dragged it as far open as he could, peering into the darkness. "It's just a book," he said, lifting out a large, flat leather volume. It was wine-colored, and the cover was cracked with age.

"A book," Jack moaned. "What good is that? Look and see if there's any money."

"There isn't, Jack," Henry told him. "Just the book." He gently set it on the counter and opened the broad cover.

The pages were lined, with neat columns, and were covered in dark, cramped script. It took Henry a minute to realize what he was looking at.

"Hey," he breathed in wonder. "I think it's the hotel's registration book. It has people's signatures and dates . . . and look! Their room numbers." Henry slid the book across the counter toward Simon and Jack. "We can see who was staying here"—he gasped—"in the 1800s!"

"Wow!" Simon exclaimed. "See when the last entry is."

Carefully, Henry turned the fragile sheets, page after page. He stared at the rows of handwritten names . . . A. J. Holman, Arthur Dimwiddy, James Bracken, Mr. and Mrs. John Perth. Finally, he came to the last page of the ledger. "It goes all the way to 1898."

He was just starting to rotate the book to show Simon, and Simon was simultaneously starting to walk around the left side of the counter to see it, when there was a low, creaking noise, followed by a loud crack.

"Simon, watch out!" Henry cried.

"No!" Jack yelled, grabbing at him.

But it was too late.

The boards gave way in a crash of splintering wood, and Simon tumbled into the blackness below.

CHAPTER 9
SIMON IN TROUBLE

HENRY AND JACK RUSHED to the edge of the shattered floorboards and squinted into the black pit.

"Simon! Simon, are you okay?" Henry called frantically.

There was silence, followed by a muted scuffling.

"SIMON!" Jack yelled.

They heard Simon groaning, then getting to his feet. "Yeah, yeah, I'm fine."

"What's down there?" Jack wanted to know. "Is it a basement?"

"I can't tell. It's too dark to see anything. It was a long way down, though! I landed on a pile of something—old sacks, I think."

"We should have brought a flashlight," Henry lamented. "But I never thought we'd need one during the daytime."

He lowered himself to his stomach, flat against the rough, gritty boards. He stretched one arm down into the darkness and waved it through the air, which felt noticeably cooler than the ground floor. "Can you reach my hand?"

Simon appeared below them, his face pale. He clambered on top of the tangle of sacks.

"I'll try," he said.

He jumped, then jumped again, swiping at Henry's outstretched hand. "I'm too far down," he said. "Let me see if there's something I can stand on."

He disappeared into the darkness, then appeared a few minutes later. "I don't see anything . . . and I don't want to go too far in the dark in case . . ." His voice trailed off, and Henry realized with a start that Simon was afraid.

"That's okay," he said quickly. "We can reach you. I'll have Jack hold my legs."

He scooted closer to the splintered hole, and Jack obligingly sat on top of his legs, while Henry privately worried that their combined weight might break through another spot in the floor. Trying not to think about that, he strained, reaching his hand as far down as he could.

"Try again," he urged Simon.

Simon jumped again and again. He piled the sacks as high as they would go and jumped from there. Then he decided the pile was too soft to allow much spring, so he pushed the sacks aside and tried jumping from the basement floor.

"Come on, higher!" Jack yelled encouragingly.

But the best Simon could do was to graze Henry's hand with his fingertips.

"It's no use," Simon said. "I can't get close enough."

Henry sat up and looked at his watch. It was eleven o'clock. They should have been on their way to Delilah's by now. "Do you think we should go for help?"

"No," Simon said firmly. "If you do, we'll never be able to come back to the ghost town again."

"Yeah, that's a terrible idea," Jack agreed.

"Besides," Simon continued, "I'm not hurt. We just have to figure out a way to get me out of this hole." He looked around. "There might be stairs or a ladder here somewhere. There should be some way to get to the main floor."

Henry could see him hesitating. "It's just so dark," Simon said. "And even if there are stairs, they're probably as rotten as the ones up there, after all these years."

"What if Henry holds on to my feet, and I hang down and grab you?" Jack suggested. "Like those trapeze guys in the circus!"

"You weigh as much as Henry. And then he'd have to pull up both of us. We're too heavy."

Henry was quite relieved to hear this plan rejected. "What if I take off my shirt and hold that down to you?" he offered. "And you grab the end, and Jack and I haul you up?"

Simon considered this, then shook his head. "I don't think it's strong enough to hold my weight. It'll rip, and I'll fall again. We need something else . . . like a rope."

"A rope!" Henry exclaimed, turning to Jack. "There was a rope near that old wagon wheel! Next to that first building, the store."

"I remember!" Jack cried. "I'll get it!" He sped from the hotel, with Henry calling after him to be careful.

Henry leaned over the hole again. "Can you see what else is down there? Anything?"

Simon shook his head. "Just these old burlap bags. But it's a pretty big room."

They lapsed into silence, waiting for Jack.

"What's that?" Simon asked suddenly, his voice thin.

"What?" Henry asked.

Simon was quiet for a second. "That noise."

Henry strained over the mouth of the hole, listening. All he could hear was Simon's quiet breathing.

"What noise?"

"Shhh," Simon said.

They both craned into the darkness. Then Henry heard it: a faint rustling in the cellar. The sound of something moving.

"Is that you?" Henry asked softly.

"No," Simon whispered.

He was quiet again. When he lifted his face to Henry, his eyes were wide with fright.

"Hen . . . there's something down here with me."

CHAPTER 10
WHAT LIES BENEATH

HENRY FELT A CHILL shoot through him.

"What do you mean? How can there be anything down there?" he asked, trying to sound normal.

But his mind was racing. He thought of the scary places in books he'd read . . . the dungeon in *The Count of Monte Cristo*, the Chamber of Secrets in the second *Harry Potter* book . . . all those dark, underground worlds where something lay waiting.

Simon shook his head, his jaw clenched. "No, it's definitely something alive. I can hear it." He was quiet again. For a minute, Henry heard only his breathing, but then the sound came again, a soft scuffling.

"Do you think it's . . . a ghost?" he asked, and then immediately wished he hadn't. He knew he'd be petrified

if he were down where Simon was, in the blackness, with something he couldn't see.

Simon's voice was a whisper. "No," he said. "It must be some kind of animal, but what could be living down here? A rat? A snake?"

Henry immediately pictured the rattlesnake pit in the book *True Grit*. "How could that be? There's no food down there."

Simon flinched. "What if I'm the food?"

There was no answer to that.

"Stay where I can see you," Henry said. He glanced over his shoulder. Where *was* Jack?

"Jack!" he yelled. "Hurry!"

Simon crouched and picked up one of the broken floorboards that had tumbled into the cellar with him. He held it grimly in both hands, like a bat.

Just then they heard footsteps outside.

"I'm coming!" Jack bellowed, and a moment later he appeared in the doorway, the old brown rope clutched in a coil against his chest.

"There's an animal or something in the basement," Henry told him quickly. "We have to get Simon out of there *now*."

"What?" Jack demanded. "What kind of animal?"

"I don't know, but we have to hurry," Henry said, throwing the rope down to Simon.

"Is it a snake?" Jack asked. "A RATTLESNAKE? I bet I will know what kind it is because of my book—"

"Jack, stop," Henry said, guiding the rope toward Simon.

Simon dropped the broken board and immediately wrapped the rope around his wrist. He gripped it with both hands.

"Okay, pull!" he cried.

Henry and Jack grabbed the rope and pulled with all their might. Simon was heavy and the angle was awkward, and the rope was so old and brittle that Henry was afraid it would fray apart in their hands. But now Simon was dangling above the basement floor, kicking his legs and trying to hoist himself up the rope. He still wasn't close enough for them to grab.

"We have to pull harder," Henry told Jack. Jack's face scrunched with the effort, turning a dark shade of red.

Now Simon was almost to the level of the splintered floorboards.

"I think I can reach you," Henry said. "But I have to let go of the rope."

"What?" Jack groaned. "I won't be able to hold it!"

"You have to!" Simon cried, panting.

"You can do it, Jack," Henry urged. "You're the strongest of all of us."

"I know," Jack said, "but Simon is HEAVY."

Henry looked quickly around. He would have to think like Uncle Hank, or like Simon himself—what was here that they could use to get Simon out of the pit?

"Wrap your end of the rope around that post by the stairs," Henry told Jack.

Jack glanced at the staircase in the corner. "That's so old. Won't it break?" he asked.

"Just try it," Henry urged.

"Hurry, guys," Simon pleaded. "I can't hold on much longer."

"Okay," Jack said. Henry gripped the rope as tightly as he could while Jack took his end and looped it twice around the post of the old staircase, cinching it. "Ready!"

"Now hold that as tight as you can, Jack," Henry told him. "And I'll bend down and pull Simon over the edge."

Quickly, Henry let go of the rope and stretched out on the rough boards, leaning out over the hole as far as he could without losing his balance. "Can you grab my hand?"

Simon nodded. He released the rope with one hand and struggled to reach up to Henry, thrashing his legs and spinning wildly over the black pit.

Henry gripped Simon's outstretched wrist. "It's okay, I've got you," he said, pulling Simon over the lip of the hole. "Okay, Jack, come help me!"

Jack ran to them, grabbing Simon's other hand, as Simon kicked free of the rope once and for all. It promptly uncoiled from the stair post and slid across the floor. They watched as its frayed length disappeared into the hole . . . joining whatever it was that lived down there.

Together, Henry and Jack hauled Simon over the edge of the broken boards, onto the floor.

Simon rolled onto his back, breathing heavily. His face was flushed with exertion.

"Thanks," he said finally.

Henry was shaking with relief, his heart still knocking furiously in his chest. He knelt at the edge of the hole and peered into the dark abyss of the cellar. Far below, he could make out the lumpy shadows of the burlap bags, crossed by a ghostly curve of rope.

"What do you think it was?" he asked softly.

"I don't know," Simon said, sitting up and rubbing his hand through his hair. "But I sure am glad I got out of there before we found out."

"Hey," Jack said. "What if it was a GHOST?" His eyes were wide.

"There's no such thing, Jack," Simon said, but Henry thought his voice lacked its usual certainty.

Jack glanced uneasily around the dark room. "You couldn't see anything but you could hear it. That sounds like a ghost. And it was coming after you! A mean ghost."

Since Henry had thought exactly this himself, it was hard to dismiss it.

But he could see that Jack was really scared. His face was pale, and his lip quivered. It was easy to forget how young Jack was, because he was so brave and sturdy all the time.

"Jack," Henry said, "I bet it was a rattlesnake."

"Really?" Jack asked hopefully. He seemed suddenly cheered.

"If it was a rattlesnake, you could have DIED," he told Simon. "And you would never have gotten out without my rope!"

"No kidding," Simon said.

Henry thought about mentioning that getting the rope had been *his* idea, but it didn't seem worth it. He sometimes wondered if the key to Jack's confidence was his ability to take credit for almost any situation. Jack was always so sure of his own importance. Whereas Henry worried constantly about screwing up—making a mistake, doing something embarrassing, getting himself or someone else into trouble—Jack had a natural inclination to see even his screwups as the linchpins of his success.

Jack stood up and brushed off his pants. "We SAVED you," he announced to Simon.

Simon smiled a little. "Yeah, you did." He took one last shuddering look down into the cellar, then got to his feet. "We'd better go. We'll have to ride like crazy to get to Delilah's by lunchtime."

"Me first!" Jack yelled, tearing out of the hotel lobby, with floorboards creaking and dust clouding the air at every step.

"I'll take the book," Henry said, picking up the ledger from the front desk and tucking it under his arm.

"Good," Simon said. "We need to have a closer look at that. Maybe if we can figure out who was staying here when it was a real gold mining town, that will be a clue to finding the Lost Dutchman's Mine."

CHAPTER 11
THE HOTEL LEDGER

THEY RODE THEIR BIKES as fast as they could over the dusty ruts back to the main road, then sped all the way back to their neighborhood. By the time they rounded the corner to Waltz Street, where Delilah lived, it was nearly twelve thirty. They could see her waiting impatiently on the front porch, her cast gleaming in the sun.

"Where were you guys?" she cried. "Your mom just called!"

"What did you tell her?" Simon asked.

"Nothing! I didn't pick up because I didn't know what to say. But you'd better call her right back."

Sweaty and panting, they burst through the front door into the cool house and ran toward the kitchen. Henry, still carrying the hotel ledger under one arm, glanced into the living room and paused. He hadn't been inside Delilah's house since their trip up the mountain, when she'd told him that her father had died several years ago in a car accident. Now, as he looked again at the cluster of photos on the end tables and the colorful array on the walls, he saw the grinning man with the kind brown eyes and felt a pang. It was strange the way a photograph could freeze someone in time, with no knowledge of the terrible things that lay ahead. There was Delilah's father holding her on his shoulders; there he was building a sand castle with her just beyond the tide line. He was smiling widely, unaware of his future. He didn't know he would never see his daughter grow up. Would he have looked different in the photos if he had known that? Henry wondered Would he have wanted to know what lay ahead?

Suddenly sad, he turned away and followed his brothers into the kitchen. While Delilah stood at the sink, filling cups with cold water, Simon took several deep breaths, then dialed the Barkers' house.

Henry, Jack, and Delilah listened anxiously to his end of the conversation.

"Hey, Mom, we're at Delilah's. You did? Sorry, we were outside . . . we didn't hear the phone. Everything's fine. You know, if you'd let me get a cell phone—yeah, I remember what you said, I just thought it would make things easier for *you*." Simon looked at Henry and rolled his eyes. "We're about to have lunch. Can we stay here for a while longer? Okay. Uh-huh. We will. Okay, Mom. Bye."

He settled the phone back in its cradle and flopped into one of the kitchen chairs with a sigh.

"Was she mad?" Jack asked.

"No, it's fine," Simon said. "She wants us home by three o'clock."

"Oh, that's PLENTY of time," Jack said happily.

"So what happened?" Delilah asked, distributing the cups. "You have to tell me! What took you so long? What did you find?"

They guzzled the water thirstily and told her all about their visit to the ghost town.

"Wow," Delilah said, turning to Simon. "I can't believe you fell through the floor! And there was something *living* down there? What do you think it was?"

"I kept thinking about that pit full of rattlesnakes in the book *True Grit*," Henry said. "With the skeletons? The girl falls in, and one bites her."

"I'm glad you didn't tell me that," Simon said in horror. "But I don't think it was a snake. I didn't hear hissing or rattling or anything. And it sounded bigger than that. Maybe it was a big ol' rat or something."

Henry thought Simon seemed quite blasé about it for someone who had been trembling with fright only an hour before.

"Well, I think it was a snake!" Jack declared. "They are tricky."

"So you didn't find anything but that book?" Delilah continued, taking the leather volume from Henry. She set it gently on the kitchen table.

"Nope, that was it," Henry told her. "But, look . . . it has the names of everybody who stayed in the hotel from 1892 to 1898." He opened the ledger and began turning the thin pages.

"Look at their funny handwriting!" Jack said. "It's all squishy."

"Yeah, it's kind of hard to read," Delilah said. "And it has the room numbers too? Was there anything left in the hotel rooms?"

"We never got that far," Simon told her. "I fell through the floor before we could go upstairs. But I doubt it. The whole town seemed to have been cleaned out."

"How does someplace become a ghost town?" Delilah wanted to know. "Do people just up and leave all at once? How come? And then it turns into a bunch of abandoned buildings?"

"Pretty much," Simon said. "But I don't think it happens all at once. It seems to mostly be mining towns that turn into ghost towns, and it's 'cuz the gold or silver or whatever they're mining runs out. So then all the businesses that used to sell stuff to miners—the stores, hotels, saloons—aren't making any money and have to close. And after a while, it doesn't make sense for anyone to live there anymore."

"When did Gold Creek shut down?" Delilah asked.

"We don't know, but it seems like the late 1800s," Simon said.

"The last hotel entry was November 5, 1898," Henry told her, shifting the hotel ledger so she could see the final page.

Delilah leaned over it, turning backward through the pages to the beginning of the book again. She ran her finger over the thin paper.

"Hey," she said suddenly. Her finger had stopped partway down the page, next to a delicate, neat black signature.

"What?" Henry asked.

"Look," Delilah said quietly.

Henry leaned over her shoulder and read:

Henry raised his eyes to Delilah's. "She is *everywhere*," he said softly.

"Julia Thomas *again!*" Jack exclaimed.

"You guys," Delilah persisted. "Look at it." She stared at the page, then at Henry.

He saw her wide eyes, and suddenly, in a flood of understanding, he knew exactly what she was thinking.

Without saying anything more, Delilah lifted her cast and plunked it on the edge of a chair.

There, gliding across the white plaster, was the librarian's signature, in neat, slanted cursive.

It looked exactly like the one in the hotel ledger.

CHAPTER 12
MORE ABOUT JULIA

"No way," Simon said.

"No way," Jack echoed.

"It's the same," Delilah said, running her finger lightly over the signature on her cast.

"It can't be," Simon said. "Unless you think the librarian is, like, a hundred and fifty years old."

Henry said nothing. He stared at the tightly curling black signature in the hotel ledger and then at its twin on the white cast. He thought of the grimly familiar face in the old photograph at the library, the name on the headstone in the old cemetery. What was going on?

"The *J*'s are the same," Delilah said stubbornly. "And the *T*'s. It's the same handwriting."

"Well, hello??? It's cursive handwriting!" Simon protested. "Nobody writes like that anymore, but back then, *everybody* did. So, I mean, signatures could look the same for that reason."

"But you just said nobody writes like that anymore," Delilah argued. "And hello, yourself—look at my cast! The librarian does write like that."

"I'm just saying there's an explanation for it. It doesn't mean that the Julia Thomas from back then is living here in Superstition right now."

Henry sank into a chair at the table and rested his face in his hands. On the other side of the kitchen window, the mountain lingered, almost as if it were peering in, enjoying their discomfort.

"You have to admit, Simon, it's pretty strange," he said. "The same name on the tombstone, the same face in the photo, and now this."

Simon leaned over Delilah's cast, shaking his head. "Yeah," he said. "I admit, it is strange. But let's try to figure out what she was doing in the hotel. Why was she there?"

"Who knows," Henry said slowly. "She had a house around here—Jacob Waltz lived with her right before he died, remember? So why would she have gone to stay in a hotel?"

"A hotel in a gold-mining town," Simon reminded them. "What's the date?"

"August 10, 1892," Henry read from the page. "She stayed in room six."

"So that was after Jacob Waltz died, right?'

Henry nodded. "That book at the library said he died in 1891. And then, remember, Julia Thomas had gotten instructions to the mine from him, or a map, and she was supposedly searching for it for years. So this would have been during that time."

Simon continued to stare at the page. "Was anybody in the room with her?"

Henry scanned the column of room numbers for August 10. "Nope," Henry said finally.

"Do you see any other names you recognize on that page?" Simon asked. "Anybody that you and Delilah read about in those books we got from the library before we went up the mountain?"

Henry squinted at the list of names covering the page. Some of the signatures were so cramped it was hard to even know what they said.

"No." He shook his head in disappointment. But then he caught his breath. "Wait . . . look! Here she is again! On September 3, in the same room, room six." It was the same slanted, decorative signature: *Julia Thomas*.

"So what does that mean?" Simon asked. "She stayed at the hotel twice, three weeks apart? I wonder why."

Delilah swung her cast off the chair and sat down next to Henry.

"We could look in that book of Arizona legends we got from the library last time," she said, "and see what it says about Julia Thomas and Jacob Waltz."

"Those are legends," Simon said doubtfully. "Made-up stuff. Does it have anything about real people?"

Delilah nodded. "That's where I read about Adolph Ruth, remember? The guy whose skull was found with two bullet holes in it, and who left that '*veni, vidi, vici*' note in his wallet?"

"Oh, yeah!" Jack exclaimed. "The same thing that was written on that teeny piece of paper in the box from Uncle Hank's desk! What did that mean again?"

"*I came, I saw, I conquered*," Henry told him. "It's Latin. Remember, back then, everyone thought it meant that Adolph Ruth had found the gold mine."

"And if Uncle Hank's note said the exact same thing, it means Uncle Hank could've found the gold mine," Jack announced.

"Right," Henry said.

But did it really mean that? There was certainly no evidence at Uncle Hank's house that he'd found a fortune in gold during his life. His house, though quirky and interesting, was very ordinary, and Henry had often heard his parents complaining since they moved in that Uncle

Hank had allowed it to fall into such disrepair. The deck had to be stained; gutters needed mending; the yard was a mess. Surely someone with a treasure's worth of gold would have built a fancy house—or at least fixed up the one he had. Or owned a fleet of cars, or bought expensive furniture, clothing, paintings, and jewelry. There was no sign that Uncle Hank had done any of these things. And yet they'd found the cryptic note at the bottom of that rust-colored metal box in his old desk, with the same Latin expression that had been on a note by Adolph Ruth.

"Let's look in my book of legends," Delilah said. "There was definitely something in there about Jacob Waltz."

She disappeared from the kitchen and returned minutes later with the book they'd checked out of the library a couple of weeks ago, before their last trip up the mountain. "I remember there was a lot about Jacob Waltz in this chapter. I didn't read all of it."

Henry secretly thought this was rather lazy of her, since he himself had thoroughly scoured the Arizona history book that was their other prize from the library that day. When she saw his withering glance, Delilah frowned at him.

"Well," she said defensively, "I was busy reading about Adolph Ruth! And like Simon said, I thought it was going to be a book of legends, not stuff that really happened. But it turns out, most of the legends started out as something true and then kind of got changed around and added to—"

"*Embellished,*" Henry said, impatient.

Delilah pursed her lips. "Whatever."

"Just see what it says about the Lost Dutchman's Mine," Simon ordered. "Is there anything about Jacob Waltz?"

Delilah turned to the index. "Here it is," she said. She flipped the pages and began reading snippets aloud. "Born in Germany . . . worked in several mines in this area . . . began looking for gold in the Superstition Mountain range in the 1870s . . . may have heard the location of a rich gold mine from an Apache Indian girl named Ken-tee."

"Indian girl?" Simon said thoughtfully.

Henry remembered reading about her in the book at the library.

Delilah's forehead wrinkled. "Ewww. It says here the tribe was so angry with her for revealing where the gold was that they cut out her tongue!"

"Yuck!" Jack made a face, wagging his tongue around. "How can you talk or eat without your tongue?"

"You can't," Simon said. "Not really. But even if some stuff is true, this is a book of legends. It's hard to know whether that really happened."

"Keep reading," Henry urged. "Does it say anything about Julia Thomas?"

"Uh-huh," Delilah murmured, turning the page. "What you already told us. Jacob Waltz got sick when his farm flooded, and she took care of him, and he supposedly gave her a map to his secret gold mine right before he died." She paused, reading silently. "And then it says she went up the mountain the following August to try to find it."

"So the timing would have been right," Simon said, running one hand through his hair. "What was the date she stayed at the hotel? August 10, 1892?" He stared at the page in the ledger. "And then again on September 3. Maybe that was on her way back."

"Wait," Delilah told them. "It says here that two men went with her, brothers from Germany." She hesitated, sliding the book toward Henry. "I don't know how you pronounce this."

Henry looked at the strange combination of letters above her finger. "Me neither," he said, struggling to wrap his mouth around the unfamiliar names. "Hermann and Rhinehart Petrasch?"

"See if those names are anywhere in the ledger for the same dates," Simon ordered.

They all leaned over the book, squinting at the faded column of signatures. Simon suddenly pressed his finger to the page. "Here! Here they are on August 10," he said. "It's hard to read, but that's the same name, right, Hen?"

Henry studied the signature above Simon's index finger. "Well, it starts with a *P*," he said, "and it ends with a *ch*."

"Yep," Simon said, "and the initials are H and R." He drew his finger horizontally across the ledger to the narrow listing of room numbers. "Look, they stayed in number five, the room next to hers."

Delilah shouldered closer to him, her brown braid brushing the page. "And on September 3, here they are again!" she said excitedly. "In the same room."

"So she went up and down the mountain with those two guys, looking for the gold mine," Simon said slowly. "The question is, did they find anything?"

He raised his head, his expression focused and serious. He was planning something, Henry could tell. It was a face he'd seen many times before.

"You know what this means, don't you?" Simon asked.

"What?" Jack asked.

"Yeah, what?" Henry echoed.

Simon took a breath. "It means that we have to go back to the ghost town. To see if Julia Thomas and those German brothers left anything behind at the hotel, in those two rooms."

CHAPTER 13
AUNT KATHY ARRIVES

"BACK TO THE GHOST TOWN? YAY!" Jack crowed. "That was fun!"

Henry stared at Simon in disbelief. "What are you talking about? You almost got eaten by something! Why would we go back there?"

"I didn't almost get eaten," Simon said dismissively. "I told you, it was probably just a rat. Also, we know what we're doing now. We'll bring flashlights and a rope, in case we run into any more trouble."

Henry shook his head. "What makes you think the hotel rooms will have anything in them? None of the other places did."

"We found the hotel guest book, didn't we?" Simon asked. "It's worth checking out—that's all I'm saying."

Delilah looked from one to the other.

"It does seem like it would be worth seeing what's in the hotel rooms, Henry," she began. "We know Julia Thomas stayed there, and we know it was right before and after she went up the mountain to search for the gold mine . . . and she seems to be the only one besides Jacob Waltz who might have known where it was."

"Yeah," Jack chimed in. "What if there's some kind of clue that would help us find the mine?"

"You're probably right," Simon said diplomatically, "that the place was cleared out long ago. But maybe the three of them left something important behind."

Henry sighed, feeling ganged up on and resentful that once again he was boxed into the role of the cautious one, rather than the fearless adventurer he wanted to be.

"When would we even do it?" He turned to Simon. "Aunt Kathy is coming in a couple of days."

Simon rubbed his forehead. "Argh. That does throw a wrench in things." He thought for a minute. "Well, maybe we can go to Gold Creek while she's here. Actually, it'll be easier to go while she's here—Mom and Dad would be way more suspicious if they saw us taking flashlights and stuff. But we won't be able to just take off on her the first day. How long are they going to be away again?"

"From Thursday till next Tuesday," Henry said.

"That's lots of time," Jack announced.

Henry worried that he was right.

The next two days were frantically busy with preparations for Aunt Kathy's visit and Mr. and Mrs. Barker's simultaneous departure. Mrs. Barker cleaned the house from top to bottom, finally unpacking the rest of the cardboard boxes and persuading Mr. Barker to hang the pictures that had been leaning against the wall of the living room since the move.

"But we haven't even talked about where they should go," Mr. Barker protested.

"I don't care where they go," Mrs. Barker replied breezily. "I just don't want Kathy to see us living in a house with big old empty walls. It's depressing."

"It will be even more depressing if I hang them in the wrong place and then we have to move them and leave a bunch of ugly holes," Mr. Barker said grimly.

Mrs. Barker threw up her hands. "Oh, just find a spot for them, Jim! I hate these bare walls. It looks like we don't intend to stay."

"Honey, Kathy knows we're staying," Mr. Barker protested. "We only moved in a month ago. She won't expect everything to be perfect."

Since Aunt Kathy was famously messy and disorganized, Henry knew that hanging the pictures could have very little to do with meeting her standards of perfection. He decided it had more to do with Mrs. Barker's need to be done with the move, once and for all. She had said many times that she was tired of spending every weekend stepping around boxes and trying to figure out the right place for a lamp or an end table from the old house.

Mr. Barker must have decided this for himself, because he relented on the pictures and spent Wednesday afternoon hanging every single one. Henry was put in charge of the ruler and pencil, and helped him line them up on the vast expanse of bare walls.

"Where are you going again?" he asked his father fretfully, thinking about the return to Gold Creek.

"Santa Fe," Mr. Barker said. He held a large framed picture against the wall, an ocean scene that had hung over the mantel in their old family room. "How's this? Is it centered?"

Henry considered. "More to the left. Where's Santa Fe?"

"In New Mexico, the next state over, up in the mountains. It should be a little cooler there."

"That'll be nice," Henry said sadly.

"What's the matter, bud?" Mr. Barker asked. He took
the pencil from Henry and marked the top of the frame.

"Oh, nothing," Henry said. "Why are you going there?"

Mr. Barker set down the picture and took the ruler,

making another mark where he intended to put the nail. "Well, your mother and I were there years ago, and we loved it. It used to be an artists' colony—do you know what that is? A place where all sorts of writers and painters went to work on their art. There are still a lot of artists living there."

Henry thought about what it would be like to live in a town filled with people who did exactly the same thing you did; who loved the same things you loved. He imagined a place full of people who read books all the time. It sounded nice, he decided. There would be so much to talk about, and you would probably like the other people because they shared your interests in the same things.

"How come they went to that place, instead of somewhere else?" he asked.

"Oh, lots of reasons." Mr. Barker held a nail against the wall and pounded it several times, hard—a sharp *bang! bang! bang!* that made Henry jump, even though he was expecting it. "It's a beautiful spot, for one thing, and the light is sharp and clear, which is what attracts painters. And the Taos Indians live nearby, and some of the artists were inspired by their culture."

Mr. Barker lifted the picture and hung it, standing

back to scrutinize the position. "Mmmm. It's a little low, maybe. What do you think?"

"It looks good," Henry told him.

"Okay, next one," Mr. Barker said, picking up a large, orange and red abstract canvas that had hung in their entryway at the old house. "Where shall we put this sucker?"

"Over there in the corner, where it's kind of dark." Henry pointed. "That painting looks like sunshine."

"Good thinking," Mr. Barker said. "It will brighten up the room." He lifted the painting and glanced over his shoulder questioningly.

"Higher," Henry said, handing him the pencil. "Why are you going away now?"

"For our anniversary." Mr. Barker scratched the pencil tip lightly against the wall.

"And you're coming back Tuesday night?"

"Yep. Around dinnertime."

Henry sighed. "But what will you do there? Without us, I mean?" It was hard to imagine how his parents could have fun without the rest of the family. He pictured them moping along the streets of a strange town, thinking of something funny to tell one of the boys and then realizing the boys were back home.

Mr. Barker grinned at him. "Oh, I don't know, Hen. It'll be pretty lonesome. But we'll come up with something to entertain ourselves."

"I don't want you to go," Henry said. He hadn't known it was true till he said it aloud, but now a heavy sense of foreboding filled him.

His father turned, hammer in hand, and studied him quizzically. "Why not, Hen? You guys will have fun with Aunt Kathy. Too much fun, probably."

Henry braced himself for the sharp crack of the hammer. "Yeah."

"Then what is it?" Mr. Barker pinched the nail between his thumb and forefinger and gave it several whacks.

"I don't know . . . ," Henry began, but at that moment, Mrs. Barker appeared in the doorway.

"Look how many you've done!" she said happily. She walked over to Henry and draped her arm over his shoulders, appraising the walls.

"That ocean painting is a little low," she said, just as Henry shot her a warning glance.

Mr. Barker spun around in exasperation, but Mrs. Barker continued smoothly, "But you know what? I like it. You guys are doing a great job." She swept quickly out of the room, calling over her shoulder, "It would be terrific if you could hang them all by dinner."

Mr. Barker rolled his eyes and lifted the orange and red canvas to hang it. Henry realized that the conversation about his parents' upcoming departure was forgotten . . . and perhaps that was for the best, since he didn't know how to explain the uneasiness he felt.

Aunt Kathy arrived on Thursday morning. Mrs. Barker picked her up at the airport, and the sisters came clattering into the house at noon, chatting and laughing and finishing each other's sentences.

"It's so good to see you!" Mrs. Barker kept saying, squeezing Aunt Kathy's arm.

"Oh, I know!" Aunt Kathy exclaimed. "I can't believe you're halfway across the country now, living in the desert."

Aunt Kathy had twinkly blue eyes and wavy light brown hair that was streaked with sunny highlights—just like her personality, Henry thought. She was bubbly and talkative and full of interesting stories. In addition to acting, which she did on the side, in community theaters and local playhouses—but which was, she would be quick to tell you, her first love—she worked for an advertising agency in Chicago. Her job was to come up with funny rhymes or slogans to sell things. Her latest project was an ad for a floral foot deodorizer, and her newest slogan was *"Put Spring in your step."*

Aunt Kathy was tired of being single and was always either madly in love or brokenhearted from a failed relationship, the details of which she never hesitated to share with the boys. She had a husky, rolling laugh that took over her entire body like a spasm. If she thought something was really funny, she would throw her head back, shoulders shaking, tears streaming down her cheeks. Then she'd breathlessly exclaim, "Oh, stop. Stop. You're killing me. I have to sit down." Finally, she'd plop into the nearest chair, shake her head, and say, "Now THAT was funny."

This whole ritual drove the boys to try to get her to laugh as often as possible.

When she came into the kitchen and saw them, she dropped her enormous purse on the floor with a thud and swept them into her arms. "Oh, my goodness, look how *big* you all are getting! Jack, you are a giant."

Jack beamed at her. "I know a lot about rattlesnakes," he told her. "Did you know their rattles are made of the same stuff as your fingernail?"

"Really?" Aunt Kathy said, glancing at her own long nails. "Isn't that interesting!"

"And when they're going to bite you—"

"Hey, buddy," Mr. Barker interrupted, "you can tell Aunt Kathy all about rattlesnakes later, okay?"

Aunt Kathy turned to Simon and Henry. "Simon— so handsome! Do you have a girlfriend yet?"

"Kathy," Mrs. Barker reproached her. "He's only in sixth grade."

"Well, that's when it starts," Aunt Kathy said cheerfully. She took Henry's face in her hands and pressed her lips to his forehead with a wet smack. "And Henry, sweetie! You have to tell me what you're reading. I finished the last of those Harry Potter books and, boy, oh boy, I thought they were fabulous. A little long by the end, but so suspenseful! I couldn't put them down."

Henry smiled up at her, and she seemed so happy and full of enthusiasm that the strange feeling of dread about his parents' departure almost vanished. But then he saw the suitcases in the hallway, and he felt it descend again.

"Okay, boys, we've got to get on the road." Mrs. Barker patted a sheaf of lined notebook paper on the kitchen table. "This is everything you need to know, Kathy.

Bedtimes, emergency numbers, doctor, dentist, vet, our hotel. We'll check in every day, and of course you can call us whenever you need us—"

"Oh, Ellen, we'll be just fine. You two go off and have a great time. Don't worry about a thing!"

Mrs. Barker hesitated, looking at the boys. "Simon, you know the house rules. I expect you all to follow them. And, Kathy, I told them they could ride their bikes around the neighborhood, but *just the neighborhood*. They need to stay close to home."

"But we can go to the library, right?" Henry asked.

Mrs. Barker pursed her lips, considering this. "I guess so. But stay on our side of Coronado Road, okay? I don't want you crossing busy streets."

"Mom, we know," Simon insisted. He flashed a secret look of triumph in Henry's direction, which Henry realized must stem from the fact that all the interesting places in town—the library, the cemetery, Emmett Trask's house, and most important, the ghost town—were on the near side of Coronado Road, so they could do all the exploring they wanted without breaking their promise to their mom not to cross the main street through town.

Mrs. Barker picked up her purse and looked at them uncertainly. "Have I forgotten anything?"

"No!" Jack told her, bouncing impatiently and looking ready to shove her out the door.

She hugged and kissed them good-bye while Mr. Barker hovered in the archway.

"Ellen, we should go. Bye, guys! Be good."

He herded their mother toward the garage, while she glanced over her shoulder and gave last-minute instructions—"Remember to feed Josie! Don't forget to use sunscreen!"

"We will," Aunt Kathy called. "We're going to have a fabulous time!"

"That's what I'm afraid of," Mrs. Barker called back, and they both started laughing.

So the mood was merry when their parents left. Even so, as Henry watched their car pull out of the driveway, he couldn't help but wonder about all that might happen before they got back.

CHAPTER 14
WHERE TO START LOOKING

THE BOYS SPENT much of the day helping Aunt Kathy "get used to Arizona," as she called it. She kept up a running commentary while they showed her around the house and yard. First of all, it was entirely too hot for her taste, and she worried that it would dry out her skin and hair. On the other hand, the sunshine was so nice, and she did like the desert, with its colorful cactuses, boulders, and wildflowers, like the stage set for a cowboy movie. The mountain was strange, though, wasn't it? She didn't like the looks of it. Did the boys hear that she'd broken up with Eddie? (The boys looked at each other blankly; they didn't even remember that she'd been dating someone named Eddie.) He was a good guy, but too immature for her taste, and she was tired of being his mother. Not that she wouldn't love to be a mother someday, but not to a grown man.

As Simon opened the door to the deck, Aunt Kathy scooped up Josie to bring her along on the rest of the "tour," much to Josie's chagrin.

"I just said to myself, 'Kathy, do you like yourself when you're with him?'" she continued. "'Do you like being the nagging, boring, responsible one all the time?'" She buried her face in Josie's soft fur. "And the answer was no. No, I did not. That's not *me*."

She picked her way across the sandy backyard in her strappy sandals, with the boys trailing behind her. When she got to the swing set, she settled herself comfortably in a swing and released Josie, who promptly streaked under the deck. "But, you see, that's the role I had to play because Eddie never took responsibility for anything. Do you know what I mean?" She glanced at Henry.

Henry nodded mutely, though truth be told, he had no idea what she was talking about. He was just relieved that Aunt Kathy seemed philosophical about this breakup. Sometimes she was so thoroughly shattered by the end of a relationship that she would be on the phone sobbing to their mother for weeks.

"So it was time to move on," she continued, twirling lazily. "Of course I miss him, because we'd gotten used to each other. But I was just completely, completely fed up with the person I'd become. I was more tired of myself than I was of Eddie!"

At this point, Aunt Kathy turned squarely to face them, planting her feet in the dust to stop the swing's motion.

"I'm telling you boys this, even though you're a little young, because it is something to think about in any relationship. Friendships too."

Simon rolled his eyes at Henry. Aunt Kathy had many, many opinions about relationships. She seemed to think the boys were old enough to hear them and to benefit somehow. When Mr. and Mrs. Barker weren't around to suggest otherwise, they had no choice but to listen.

"Think of your friends," Aunt Kathy said. "You should ask yourself, does this person bring out the best in me? Do they like me for the things I like most about myself? Do they support me and stick up for me? Do they push me in new directions?"

"My friends had better not push ME," Jack declared. "Or I will push them back."

Aunt Kathy laughed her big, rolling laugh, and the swing shuddered. "Not that kind of pushing, sweetie," she said. "I mean, do they open up new worlds for you, challenge you to try new things? Those are the important questions. Some of my women friends have this long list of characteristics they're looking for in a guy—athletic, tall, ambitious, good job—and I'm like, 'Honey, those things don't matter at all compared with how he treats you. How he makes you feel. How you are when you're with him.'"

Simon and Henry exchanged glances.

"I think we'll go for a bike ride," Simon announced. "Is that okay? As long as we're home for dinner?"

"Oh, I'm sorry! I'm talking your ears off, aren't I? I'm just so excited to see you boys, that's all." She grabbed Henry and squeezed him tightly against her side, until he could feel the rope of the swing cutting into his chest. "I feel like it's been forever. Of course you can go for a bike ride. What was I supposed to remind you about again?"

"To stay in the neighborhood," Henry volunteered.

"And put on sunscreen," Simon added.

"See how responsible you boys are? Why, you're better than Eddie. All right, be back in a couple of hours, by dinner time. I thought we'd just have pizza. But I'll make fudge sauce, and we can have sundaes for dessert."

"That sounds *delectable*," Henry said.

Aunt Kathy smiled at him. "Henry. You and your words."

"It sounds GREAT," Jack shouted, throwing his arms around her shoulders and sending the swing spinning wildly.

Minutes later, they quickly slathered themselves with sun lotion and hopped on their bikes.

"Where are we going?" Jack asked, pedaling ahead of them.

"Let's ride over to Delilah's," Simon said. "We can talk about where to start looking for the gold."

Delilah swung open the door with a scowl. "I thought you guys were never going to get here!" she said. "What took so long?"

"Aunt Kathy came," Henry told her. "We had to get her settled."

"Did you ask her what 'break a leg' means?" Delilah asked, thumping back to the kitchen on her cast.

"Shoot, we forgot," Simon said.

"You can ask her when you meet her," Henry added.

"When am I going to meet her?" Delilah asked.

"Anytime you want. She's at our house for six whole days, till next week," Henry said. "You'll like her." He was suddenly sure that was true, though he couldn't say why.

Jack tugged open the refrigerator and inspected the contents. "Don't you have soda?"

Delilah shook her head. "My mom says it's bad for your teeth."

Jack sighed. "That's what our mom says. I thought maybe your mom didn't know that."

"There's iced tea," Delilah offered. "With sugar and lemon."

She lined up four glasses on the counter and took a yellow plastic pitcher from the refrigerator, pouring carefully.

Henry looked out the kitchen window, at the dark silhouette of Superstition Mountain, like a thundercloud gathering in a clear sky. Was there really a cavern full of gold hidden somewhere in its canyons?

"So when are we going back to the ghost town?" Simon asked.

"*We* aren't," Delilah said dejectedly. "*You* are. I can't go anywhere with this thing."

Even though he had envied her the excuse to avoid Simon's risky schemes, Henry felt sorry for her. That cast made it hard for Delilah to choose adventure even if she wanted to. "Hey," he said suddenly. "We could go to Emmett's. And Delilah could come too."

"Emmett's?" Simon turned to him. "Why would we go back there?"

"Well, he's a geologist, right?" Henry said. "He knows

about different kinds of rocks. And he had all those survey maps of the mountain, remember? Maybe he could help us figure out where the gold is likely to be—in what part of the mountain. You know?"

Simon considered this for a minute. "That's not a bad idea," he said slowly. "In fact, it's a pretty good idea, Hen." He clapped Henry's shoulder. "It would be better not to go back to Gold Creek for a couple of days anyway, because of Aunt Kathy getting used to things."

"I can't ride my bike," Delilah said doubtfully. "And Emmett's house is too far away to walk."

"Oh, Aunt Kathy will drive us," Simon said confidently. "We can go tomorrow. I don't think he'll mind talking to us. He was president of the historical society, after all. He might know something about the Julia Thomas—the old Julia Thomas, not the librarian—that would help us find the gold."

What if the old Julia Thomas IS the librarian? Henry was thinking. But he was looking forward to seeing Emmett, who was a font of interesting information about Superstition Mountain and all that had happened there.

CHAPTER 15
SOMETHING AMISS

THE NEXT MORNING, it was surprisingly easy to persuade Aunt Kathy to drive them to Emmett's house. Simon made a phone call first, to find out if Emmett was there. According to Simon, though Emmett was surprised to hear from them—"Oh, you guys! Of course I remember you. What's up?"—he seemed very amenable to answering more questions about the geology of the mountain . . . perhaps because Simon said nothing of gold mines or buried treasure. But Emmett had a meeting at one o'clock in Phoenix, so they would have to go over that morning.

"We can pick up Delilah on the way," Henry told Aunt Kathy.

She was leaning over the dresser in their parents' bedroom, using the mirror to apply lush sweeps of mascara. "The little girl who found Josie?"

Henry almost said, *The little girl who* took *Josie.* "Yeah," he said. "She broke her leg."

"I know." Aunt Kathy dusted her cheeks with blush. "Your mother told me about that. And whose house are we going to?"

"Emmett Trask's," Henry told her. "He used to be head of the historical society here." This made Emmett sound more legitimate, he thought.

Aunt Kathy raised an eyebrow. "The historical society? That doesn't sound like something that would interest you boys. Why are we going to his house?"

"Well," Henry said, "he knows a lot about the history of the town, so we wanted to ask him a few things. And he's a geologist, so he knows about rocks and stuff."

"Hmm, he sounds smart." Aunt Kathy shrugged. "Okay, I'm game."

Delilah was sitting on the curb in the bright sun when they pulled into her driveway. She hobbled quickly to the car and climbed in the backseat.

"Hi," she said to Aunt Kathy. "I'm Delilah."

"It's nice to meet you, honey. I'm Kathy, Ellen's sister. I've heard all about you. You look like an old pro with that cast—how long till it comes off?"

"At least a couple more weeks," Delilah said. She lifted her leg toward the driver's seat. "Can you see what Mr. Barker wrote on it?" she asked, turning the cast slightly.

Aunt Kathy squinted. "Oh! Break a leg!" She laughed.

"He told us it's something actors say. He thought you might know why."

Aunt Kathy backed the car out of the driveway, smiling. "Well, I should—I've been doing theater since high school! But I'm not sure anyone knows exactly where it comes from. One theory is that 'break a leg' is an expression for bending your knees when you bow or curtsy . . . so to 'break a leg' would be to perform so well you get to take lots of bows. Another theory, kind of similar, is that it refers to curtain calls. Do you know what those are?"

Simon answered from the passenger seat. "It's when they open the curtains again and again at the end of a show, so the actors can take an extra bow."

"Right," Aunt Kathy said. "In the theater, the curtains used to be held up by wooden pieces called 'legs,' and to open the curtains, you had to 'break' the legs. So 'break a leg' could mean to open the curtains a bunch of times, or to wish an actor lots of curtain calls."

Delilah smiled, satisfied. "Mr. Barker said you would know."

They reached Emmett's road moments later. "Wow, this is out in the middle of nowhere," Aunt Kathy said as she turned the car down the rutted lane. "Oh! And there's the mountain again." She shuddered. "There's no escaping that thing."

Henry saw that it completely filled the windshield, a looming presence. They bounced and bumped directly toward it until they finally reached Emmett's long gravel drive, with the white house and red pickup truck waiting at the end.

Before Aunt Kathy had even turned off the engine, Jack flung open the car door and scampered up the front steps. "Emmett!" he yelled, pounding on the door.

Henry wondered briefly if it was okay to call him that instead of Mr. Trask. But he did seem more like an Emmett than a Mr. anybody. He wasn't as old as their parents, for one thing, and he was oddly direct when he talked to them, as if they were grown-ups too.

Henry, Simon, and Delilah followed Jack, while Aunt Kathy gathered her bag and set one sandaled foot gingerly on the loose stones.

Emmett opened the door and grinned at them. "Hey, you guys," he said easily. "Come on in." He hesitated. "Is that your mom?"

Aunt Kathy slammed the car door shut, tossed her hair over her shoulder, and flashed him a wide smile. "Oh, no," she said. "My sister's the married one. I'm the fun one! I'm taking care of them for a few days while their parents are in Santa Fe." She walked toward the front stoop, extending her hand. "Kathy McCarthy."

"Oh." Emmett didn't seem to know what to say, but he took her hand. "Emmett Trask." He held the door wide while Aunt Kathy beamed at him and breezed into the house.

"The boys told me you're a geologist! I bet that is very interesting work. Especially in this part of the country. There are rocks everywhere!"

Henry thought this was a goofy thing to say; in what part of the country *weren't* there rocks everywhere? The whole country was made of rocks. But Aunt Kathy seemed not the least bit bothered by her own ignorance.

"What a cozy house!" she said enthusiastically. "Look at that wonderful map."

"It's a survey map of Superstition Mountain," Henry

told her. His eyes scanned the soft pastels of the map, thickly covered in wavy lines. Did it hold some clue to the location of the gold mine?

"Here, sit down." Emmett gestured to a lumpy tan couch and a couple of armchairs before sitting down himself.

Aunt Kathy immediately plopped down, crossing her legs and beckoning for Henry to sit next to her.

"What can I do for you guys?" Emmett asked.

"Well," Simon began, "we found out something interesting. There was a woman named Julia Thomas who used to live near Superstition a long time ago . . . when Jacob Waltz was alive."

"With the same name as the library lady! And looks exactly like her too!" Jack blurted out.

Emmett seemed amused. "It was Julia Schaffer, actually—is that who you mean? She was a friend of Jacob Waltz."

"No!" Jack corrected. "Julia THOMAS."

"Now, who are you all talking about?" Aunt Kathy asked.

Delilah lowered herself to the carpet at Aunt Kathy's feet, her cast stretched out in front of her, and began to explain. "Jacob Waltz was a miner who lived near

Superstition in the 1880s," she said. "He was German, but people thought he was Dutch, and he discovered a big gold mine on the mountain that people call the Lost Dutchman's Mine, because nobody has ever been able to find it again."

"Gold?" Aunt Kathy exclaimed. "Right here? On Superstition Mountain?" She glanced out the living room window at the hulking, craggy shape of the mountain. "It does look mysterious, doesn't it? It's so *dark*, even on this sunny day."

"The mine is supposed to have the richest vein of gold in the entire U.S.," Simon told her. Turning back to Emmett, he said, "The woman we read about had the same name as the librarian. Not Schaffer, Thomas. We thought it was kind of an interesting coincidence."

"*And* her grave is at the cemetery," Henry added. Which was more than a coincidence, and more than interesting . . . it was spooky.

Aunt Kathy shuddered. "What were you boys doing at the cemetery? That doesn't seem like a very fun place to play. Did you remember to hold your breath?"

Jack looked at her appreciatively. "I tried," he began, and Henry shot him a warning glance, sorry that he'd brought up the cemetery. Their parents didn't know they'd gone to that place and certainly didn't know what they'd found there. But Jack continued obliviously, "But then we were there for *sooooo* long—"

Simon interrupted smoothly, "We thought you might know about her, Emmett, because of the historical society and all."

"Yes, I know a bit," Emmett said. "Let's see what I can tell you about Jacob Waltz and anybody named Julia." He took a battered volume off the bookshelf and thumbed through it. Henry read the faded title: *The Lost Dutchman's Mine: History and Legend.*

"Here we go," Emmett said after a few minutes.

"Is she in there?" Henry asked. "Julia Thomas?"

He nodded, reading to himself. "Her name *was* Julia Thomas, before she married Albert Schaffer. I think of her as Julia Schaffer, but you're right, her original name was the same as the librarian's. Is this the woman you're thinking of—the one who took care of Jacob Waltz when he was ill?"

"Yes," Henry said. "She was with him when he died."

Delilah leaned forward eagerly. "Supposedly, he gave her a map . . . or at least directions to his gold mine."

Aunt Kathy sighed. "How romantic! Did she ever find it?"

"No, that's the local lore," Emmett said quickly. "I

don't know how much of it is true. And I don't think they were romantically involved. . . ." He stopped, his cheeks reddening slightly.

Aunt Kathy seemed unperturbed. "Well, it's hard to know what was going on between two people so long ago.

And it's still a romantic story! She cared for him till he died and then he gave her the map to his gold mine." She laughed. "No guy has ever given me anything nearly that interesting."

"What's 'lore'?" Jack demanded.

"Stories that people pass down, from generation to generation," Henry told him.

"Julia was quite the businesswoman," Emmett said. "When she was unsuccessful locating the mine herself, she made a living—"

"Selling copies of the map," Simon interjected.

"Yes, to the local gold hunters." Emmett's mouth twisted in disgust. "They were all stricken with gold fever, from what I can tell . . . like the other Julia Thomas and the rest of those folks in the historical society."

"What's gold fever?" Jack asked. "Is it something you catch?"

Emmett and Aunt Kathy exchanged glances and laughed.

"No," Emmett said. "At least not the way you catch a disease. It's more like an obsession. All the person can think about is gold—how to get it, how to keep other people from getting it first."

"During the Gold Rush, it was common, wasn't it?" Aunt Kathy asked him. "People were so driven." And as Emmett nodded, she told the boys, "With gold fever, gold becomes the single point of focus for someone, more important than anything else in life. Like any addiction."

"It really was an addiction," Emmett agreed. "People caught up in gold fever spent every last dime, lost their homes and families, all for the sake of their dream of striking it rich."

Simon considered this, rubbing his hand through his hair. "But if so many people were looking, and for so many years, why didn't they ever find the gold?"

Emmett sighed. "Is this really what you guys want to talk about? The gold? You should go to a meeting of the historical society."

"With that mean librarian?" Jack protested. "No way!"

Emmett smiled. "Yeah, you're right. She is kind of mean." He ran his hand through his hair and Henry saw his expression soften, the way their mother's did when she was about to change her mind.

"So how come nobody ever found the gold?" Henry asked, echoing Simon.

Emmett shrugged. "Lots of reasons. Maybe the gold never existed to begin with. Or Jacob Waltz mined it until the reserves were depleted. Or the mine is so well hidden it will never be found. Or the map that Julia Thomas circulated was a hoax." His mouth curved in a half smile. "Or, if you accept the Apache explanation, the Thunder God took his revenge and made sure treasure seekers looking for the gold paid a price. Sometimes with their very lives."

"The Thunder God?" Simon asked. "What the heck is that?"

Thunder God. Henry stared out Emmett's window at the shadowy slopes of Superstition Mountain. Despite the heat of the day, he shivered. Was that why the mountain felt alive? Like it was always watching them?

"Don't worry, it's not real," Emmett said quickly. "Just part of the Apache belief system. The Thunder God is the god of the mountain. According to legend, he protects it from intruders. I imagine the name comes from the severe electrical storms and thunderstorms we have in this area, especially during the summer months. The storms are so loud and violent, the Indians saw them as evidence of divine power."

The Thunder God might not be real, Henry thought,

but it seemed as good an explanation as any for the mysterious happenings on the mountain.

Emmett returned to the book, reading silently. "Anyway, Julia Thomas sold maps or directions to the mine for years. And then remarried and became Julia Schaffer."

"You know what's strange?" Simon said after a minute. He looked at Henry, his brow furrowed. "The tombstone in the cemetery . . ."

Henry could picture it, old and cracked, with the name in faded letters. He knew what Simon was about to say.

Simon continued in bewilderment, "It said Julia Thomas. Not Julia Schaffer."

Delilah got to her feet. "That's right. Why would that be? Did she keep her maiden name or something?"

"No," Emmett said. "I've read about her as Julia Schaffer. You must be wrong about the tombstone."

"No, we're not," Simon said firmly. "We all saw it."

"Yeah, me too!" Jack piped up.

Henry and Delilah stared at each other, nodding mutely.

Emmett frowned, scanning the open book. "But she wasn't even buried here in Superstition. Julia Schaffer moved to Phoenix with her husband."

"Maybe she came back," Henry suggested. "At the end

of her life?" It still didn't explain why the name on the tombstone was Thomas.

"No," Emmett said. He turned *The Lost Dutchman's Mine* toward Henry and tapped the middle of the page with his finger. "It says here that they joined some mystical religious group. They had fire pits burning on their property all the time. Julia Schaffer died and was buried there . . . in Phoenix."

Simon, Henry, Jack, and Delilah all looked at each other.

"Then who's in Julia Thomas's grave at the cemetery?" Delilah asked.

CHAPTER 16
GOLD ORE AND LORE

"HOLD ON," EMMETT SAID. "You haven't convinced me there IS a Julia Thomas grave at the cemetery . . . or even if there is, that it has anything to do with this Julia. I'll have to go over there and have a look sometime."

"Sometime?" Jack protested, incredulous. "We should go NOW! We'll prove it to you."

Henry was inclined to agree. He pictured the tilting headstone. If the real Julia Thomas wasn't buried in that grave, then who was?

"Oh, sweetie, I'm sure Emmett has better things to do with his day than poke around an old cemetery," Aunt Kathy interjected. "He's been nice enough to let you come over and ask him all these questions." She flashed another big smile at Emmett, who looked startled by her attention.

"It's not that," he said evenly. "I have a meeting in Phoenix this afternoon, so there's no way I can do it today. Maybe over the weekend."

Henry sighed. In his experience, the weekend was a black hole of adult promises that rarely came to fruition. "Well," he began, "if we can't figure out anything more about Julia Thomas right now, maybe you could tell us about the geology of the mountain?"

Emmett's face lit up. "Sure! What do you want to know? How it was formed? How it's changing? The different kinds of rock?"

"No, not that stuff," Jack said. "We want to know where the GOLD is!"

"Jack," Simon rebuked, turning to Emmett. "We're interested in anything you can tell us about the mountain."

Aunt Kathy added quickly, "Of course we are! I think it's just fascinating that you know so much about it."

Henry stared at her. Why was she acting so strange and . . . sparkly? With an inward groan, he suddenly realized that she liked Emmett and wanted him to like her back.

Simon continued, "And where you think the gold might be . . . from your work as a geologist."

Emmett let out an aggrieved sigh and studied the ceiling. "Come on, you guys, think about what we've just been discussing. People have been searching for the Lost Dutchman's Mine ever since Waltz died—for over a century. They haven't found anything."

"But you just said that could be because it's so well hidden," Delilah pointed out.

"Or because it doesn't exist!" Emmett countered. "That's the most likely explanation."

Henry tried a different tack. "We thought you might know which areas of the mountain were the most likely . . . ," he began, but in the face of Emmett's obvious frustration, his voice faltered. "The places with the best chance of having gold," he ended weakly.

"How does the gold get there, anyway? Can you tell us that?" Simon asked.

That seemed something Emmett was more willing to discuss. He leaned forward in his chair. "Well, gold deposits can accumulate in lots of different geological environments," he began. "Old volcanoes, hot springs, or sandstone or conglomerates—those are mixes of different kinds of rock—when they weather and erode. One of the most common places for gold to form is in ancient fault zones, where earthquakes once happened . . . two and a half billion years ago, during the Archean period."

"Two and a half *billion*?" Simon said. "That's a *really* long time ago."

"Before the dinosaurs?" Jack asked.

"Way before that," Simon scoffed.

"Right," Emmett continued. "The earthquakes that happened along these giant faults—cracks in the earth's surface—were accompanied by a release of hot liquids from deep in the earth's crust. The solutions moved upward along the cracks, bubbling to the surface like the fizz in a bottle of soda when you open it. That process resulted in gold forming in veins of rock."

"But what IS the gold?" Henry asked. "Is it just another kind of rock? It sounds all liquidy when you describe it."

"Gold is an element," Emmett said. He raked one hand through his hair, and Henry could tell he was trying to think of a simpler way to explain it. "Inside the earth—under the thin, hard crust on the surface—there's a layer that's molten, so it *is* liquid."

"Under the ground is liquid?" Jack exclaimed. "So we're walking around on top of liquid?" He jumped to his feet and stomped hard on Emmett's floor. "Cool!"

"No—hot," Emmett corrected him. "Very hot. That's what *molten* means."

"Jack, careful," Aunt Kathy said. "You don't want to mark up Emmett's floor."

Molten. Henry whispered the word to himself. He loved the kind of word that sounded like what it was—and this one sounded liquidy and hot and moving. Like lava.

Emmett was lost in thought, talking about what went on deep below the earth's crust. "The molten goo is full of elements," he said, "and most elements like to form compounds with other elements. When they do that and cool down, near the surface of the earth, they become rocks or ores. But gold isn't like that. It doesn't like to form compounds; it's attracted to other particles of gold more than to any other element. So it stays pure, which is one reason it's so valuable. It forms nuggets or veins of pure gold metal. Does that make sense?"

"Like soul mates," Aunt Kathy said, and smiled.

Henry stared at her. Why was she being so goofy? And why was Emmett blushing like that?

Emmett's cheeks flushed, and he cleared his throat. "Well, I'm not sure that's the comparison I'd make—"

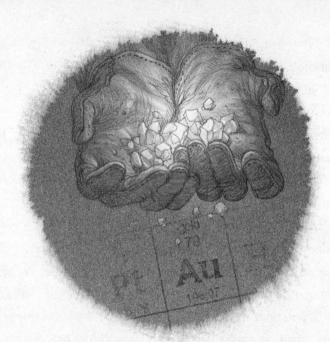

Simon ignored this exchange. "So it's like the way metal is attracted to a magnet, but gold is only attracted to itself," he said thoughtfully. "But what does that tell you about *where* the gold might be on Superstition Mountain?"

Emmett jumped up and walked over to the survey map on the wall. With one finger, he traced an area on the right side of the map.

"Well, we know the location of some of the faults. We can compare those locations to the documented history of gold mining on the mountain, to the places where gold has actually been found. The Spanish discovered silver and gold ore in Arizona a few centuries ago, but the first evidence of *mining* on the mountain wasn't until the 1800s."

"Okay, okay," Jack said impatiently. "So where's the gold?"

Emmett continued to circle a peach-colored part of the map with his finger. "The most likely place is here. By Weaver's Needle."

Jack raced across the room, and Henry and Simon quickly followed. Even Aunt Kathy stood up, tilting her head to one side as she studied the map. They all clustered around Emmett, peering past his fingertip at a pale orange area that was densely covered in elevation lines.

"You think that's where the gold is?" Simon asked.

Emmett nodded. "Listen: as I said before, I'm not convinced there's any left. But if there is, I think it would be somewhere over here." He paused, tapping his finger. "Most likely in one of these little hidden canyons."

CHAPTER 17
MAKING A DATE

HENRY CAUGHT HIS BREATH. He thought of the secret canyon that he'd discovered while he and Delilah were waiting to be rescued, the one that was marked on the old map they'd found in the saddlebag. He remembered squeezing through the rock passageway into the narrow gorge, with its high walls and thin strip of blue sky overhead. Was the entrance to the Lost Dutchman's Mine somewhere in that canyon? He looked at Simon, eyes wide, and Simon returned a quick, sharp glance.

"The people who've been looking for the gold all these years," Simon said slowly. "Do you think they've been searching that part of the mountain?"

Emmett shrugged. "In a hundred and fifty years? The treasure hunters have looked all over the place. But the mountain has so many canyons and ravines, and some of them are so remote and difficult to access, it's unlikely they've all been explored."

Aunt Kathy lifted her hair off her neck and twisted it into a ponytail, deftly sliding an elastic band over it. "What about the map you mentioned? That the Waltz fellow supposedly gave his girlfriend? Did it show the gold mine to be in that area?"

Emmett shook his head impatiently. "First of all, she wasn't his girlfriend. Second of all, we don't know if he gave her a map or just verbal or written directions to the mine. Julia did have a map that she made copies of and sold to tourists and gold hunters, but I'm not sure any copies of it have survived. I've never seen one."

"Hmmm," Aunt Kathy said, still squinting at the map. "What would an old gold mine look like, anyway?"

"That's the problem," Emmett said. "It might not look like much of anything—just a hole in the ground or the rock, generally not big enough for a man to stand in. And rock slides are such a common thing on the mountain— lots of those mine entrances get buried eventually. I've heard stories that back in the 1800s, when there was an avalanche, some of the miners were trapped inside them."

"Really?" Henry asked, horrified. "Buried alive?"

"Yes," Emmett nodded grimly. "You don't get much

warning of an avalanche, usually. You'll start to hear the rumble of rocks falling, but they can come down so thick and fast there's no time to escape."

"And people can't dig their way out?" Delilah asked. "When the rock slide is over?"

"It depends. If it's just a few rocks, sure. But if it's a massive rock slide, no. The rocks are too heavy to move."

It would be like a rocky tomb, Henry thought. Sort of like a mausoleum, but the people inside would still be *alive*. He shuddered.

Delilah shook her head determinedly, as if shaking the image out of her mind. "But what about the mine entrances that weren't buried by rock slides? Do they just look like holes?"

Emmett nodded. "Sometimes the entrance would have been reinforced with wood beams, but often it was just dug out, like a tunnel. And the prospector would have good reason to keep it hidden."

"*Camouflaged*," Henry said thoughtfully.

"What's that mean?" Jack asked.

"You know, like army uniforms," Henry told him. "Blending in."

Simon flattened his hand on the map over the peach-colored area of the map. "So you think even if the treasure hunters did explore these little canyons, they could have missed the entrance to the mine?"

"Sure," Emmett said. He glanced at his watch. "I'm sorry, guys, but I need to get my stuff together and head into Phoenix."

"Oh, we stayed too long!" Aunt Kathy exclaimed. "I'm sorry, I wasn't paying attention to the time."

"No, it's okay," Emmett said quickly. "I'm glad you came." He smiled at Kathy. "It was nice to meet you."

Uh oh, Henry thought, *don't encourage her.* But it was too late. Aunt Kathy's whole face lit up, glowing warmly at him as she herded the boys and Delilah toward the door. "And I am just so happy I got to meet *you*," she gushed, touching Emmett's arm. "I've never been to this part of the country before, so this is all new to me. It's fascinating to hear an . . . *expert* . . . talk about the environment and history of this place. I wish I could have you as a tour guide while I'm here!" She laughed, hiking her purse strap over her shoulder and stepping onto the porch.

Delilah looked at Henry and raised her eyebrows slightly. All Henry could do was shrug.

Emmett held the door wide for them. "Oh . . . ," he said slowly, and Henry saw that he was blushing again.

He looked down, as if embarrassed. It reminded Henry of what he himself did when he was daydreaming in class and the teacher called on him and he had no idea what to say. But how could a grown-up be like that? Surely after you'd lived all those years, you would have things figured out. He glanced at Aunt Kathy, who was watching Emmett with a shy, twinkly look. Henry decided they were as silly and awkward as any kids he'd ever met.

"Well, I'd be happy to show you around, if you like," Emmett said. "How long are you here?"

Aunt Kathy hesitated on the porch, shielding her eyes from the bright sun as she smiled up at him. "Just until Tuesday, when the boys' parents get back from Santa Fe. Would you have time this weekend maybe? I'd love that."

Emmett paused. "Sure. Sunday? I can give you a sense of the desert, and there are some Indian petroglyphs about an hour's drive from here." Warming up, he added, "I'll show you the most interesting rock formations in the area." With a twinge of resentment, Henry noticed that this offer sounded much more specific—on the verge of becoming an actual *plan*—than Emmett's earlier comment about visiting the cemetery.

"Oh, that would be wonderful!" Aunt Kathy fumbled briefly in her purse and scribbled something on a torn piece of paper. "Here's my cell," she said. "Call me, and we'll figure out a time. I just have to check with my sister to make sure the boys can be on their own for a bit."

"Oh." Emmett paused. "Well, I could take all of you. I'd be happy to."

Before the boys could even muster a reply, Aunt Kathy jumped in. "That's very sweet of you, but the boys don't like long car rides, do you?" She shot Henry a pointed glance.

"And we'll have chores to do on Sunday," he chimed in helpfully.

"What chor—" Jack began to protest, but Simon subtly punched him in the back before he could finish.

"So let me make sure it's okay with their parents, and we'll set up a time, okay?" Aunt Kathy continued. "Thank you so much, Emmett! This will be the highlight of my trip." She tousled Henry's hair and remembered to add, "Next to seeing my nephews, of course."

After they all got into the car and Aunt Kathy was backing it out of the driveway, she told them cheerily, "Now, see? I have a date! That, my friends, is how it's done."

"Oh, brother," Simon muttered, shaking his head.

But Henry could tell from his expression that he was thinking the same thing Henry was: Aunt Kathy was going to be busy all day on Sunday, which meant they were going to be left on their own.

When they reached Delilah's house, Aunt Kathy pulled the car up to the curb to let her out.

"I'm so glad I got a chance to meet you," she told Delilah. "I hope your leg will be better soon."

"You don't have to say good-bye," Simon said. "You'll see her again. We hang out with her all the time."

Delilah smiled at him, and Henry felt a small pang. Simon always seemed to know the perfect thing to say. While Henry agonized over seeming too pushy or too eager or just plain rude, Simon said what he was thinking, and it always seemed to come out exactly right.

Delilah started to get out of the car, then stopped. "Hey, what's my bike doing there?"

Henry saw that her bike was in the driveway, leaning against the garage door.

"You must have left it there," he said.

She shook her head. "No, I didn't. I haven't ridden my bike since I broke my leg. It's been in the garage the whole time."

"Did you leave your garage open?" Aunt Kathy asked.

Delilah frowned. "Sometimes the side door is unlocked."

"Is your mother home?"

"No, she's at work."

Aunt Kathy shifted the car into park. "Boys, help her put the bike back. I'll have a look around and make sure it's safe for her to go in the house."

The boys climbed out and dutifully followed Delilah up the driveway. Simon walked to the side of the garage and turned the handle on the door, which opened easily. "It's unlocked," he said, and then, "Wow! Look at all the cool camping stuff. I'm surprised somebody didn't take that."

"That's my dad's," Delilah said, and Henry remembered the silver compass, Delilah's prized possession that she'd said was from camping trips with her dad . . . now lost somewhere on the mountain.

"Hey," Jack interrupted, "there's Josie."

And there, indeed, was Josie, crouched in one of the landscaped beds near the front porch. She gazed at them calmly, one ear twitching.

"I wonder if she saw who was fooling around with my bike," Delilah said.

Henry felt suddenly sure that Josie *had* seen it. But Josie was so implacable, she would look exactly the same whether she'd seen something suspicious or not.

"Well, is your bike okay?" Simon asked her. "They didn't do anything to it, did they?"

Delilah hobbled over to the bike and leaned down,

scrutinizing the tires. "It looks fine—" She stopped. "There's something in the basket."

Henry peered over her shoulder into the bike's white wicker basket. There was a folded slip of paper at the bottom. Delilah pinched it between her fingers and took it out, opening it carefully.

Jack pushed next to her, leaning close to the note. "Who's it from? What does it say?"

Delilah's brow furrowed. She held the note out to Henry. Neat capital letters in black felt tip crossed the white paper. Henry stared at Delilah. Quietly, he read aloud: "What was in the saddlebag doesn't belong to you."

CHAPTER 18
SECRET LETTERS

SIMON SNATCHED THE PAPER and read it for himself. "I thought you said nobody knew about the saddlebag," he said to Henry. "You said you hid it."

"I did," Henry protested. "I did hide it! When Delilah and I were alone in the canyon." He turned to her for support, and she nodded at Simon.

"We didn't tell anybody about it, not even the police," Delilah said. "That's why we hid it! So we wouldn't have to carry it all the way down the mountain, and so nobody would know about it."

"Jack!" Simon whirled around. "Did you say something—"

"NO!" Jack shouted. "You are always blaming me! That was a SECRET, and I didn't—"

"What's going on?" Aunt Kathy called, walking toward them from the house. "What are you arguing about?"

"Nothing," Simon said quickly, jamming the paper into his pocket.

"Is everything okay?" She looked from one of them to the other. "Delilah, is anything wrong with your bike?"

Delilah shook her head. Henry thought she looked pale, and her freckles stood out even more than usual.

Aunt Kathy glanced back at the house. "Well, honey, the doors are locked, and it doesn't look like anyone's been inside. Give me the key, and I'll go in with you. Henry, put her bike back in the garage."

Delilah roused herself from her daze and took out her house key. "Hang on," she said to Henry. "I'll put up the garage door."

She and Aunt Kathy disappeared into the house, and a minute later, the garage door lifted, clattering on its metal tracks. Henry rolled the bike into the garage, past a folded tent, tarps, and several complicated-looking backpacks with straps and clips dangling from them. He thought about the note. What did it mean? Who could have been watching them in the canyon? The only possibility, he realized with a shudder, was whoever had been shooting at them.

"The house is fine," Aunt Kathy called.

Jack ran to the front steps and scooped up Josie, whose ears flattened in protest. Delilah stood in the doorway uncertainly.

"Alrighty, boys, back in the car," Aunt Kathy said. She rested one hand on the driver's-side door, studying Delilah. "Will you be okay here, hon? When does your mother get home?"

"Yeah, I'm fine. She'll be home by five or so."

Aunt Kathy seemed unconvinced. "Would you rather come back with us until then?"

"That's okay," Delilah said.

Henry turned to her. "You might as well," he urged. "We'll probably want you to come over later anyway." He knew Simon was going to want to look at the old map again, after the conversation with Emmett. Besides, even if the note wasn't exactly a threat, somebody had been at Delilah's house, messing with her things. It was unsettling.

She hesitated for only a second. "Okay," she said, and Henry could hear the relief in her voice. She pulled the door shut behind her and carefully locked it.

On the way back to their house, they had to listen to Aunt Kathy chatter excitedly about Emmett. Wasn't he the nicest man? So smart and interesting. Maybe not *traditionally handsome*, but he had the cutest smile. She could never resist a cute smile. Now, you did have to wonder about somebody living all by himself like that, out in the middle of nowhere. That wasn't a good sign— "a red flag," Aunt Kathy called it.

"He doesn't have any flags," Jack corrected her. "Just rocks."

Aunt Kathy laughed her rolling laugh. "No, sweetie, it's an expression. A red flag is a warning sign . . . but, I don't know, he is a scientist. They're different. Maybe in his case, living alone in the boonies isn't a red flag." This prompted a discourse about scientists and their quirks. In Aunt Kathy's experience, they could be nerdy loners. But they were usually honest and straightforward, and they weren't afraid of commitment. Better that than a player, in Aunt Kathy's opinion.

Henry was only half listening to her, but he perked up when he heard the word "player." It was the term their mother often used disapprovingly to describe Uncle Hank in his relationships with women.

"That's what Mom says Uncle Hank was," he told Aunt Kathy. "What does it mean exactly?"

Aunt Kathy thought for a minute. "Well, a player is a lady's man . . . somebody with a lot of different girl-friends and nobody special."

"Is it a bad thing?" Henry asked.

"It doesn't sound bad for the guy," Simon observed.

Aunt Kathy considered. "I think it depends on what you're looking for. It's all about expectations, you know? If a woman wants a casual, easy relationship with a guy and isn't expecting anything more, then a player might be just fine."

This made absolutely no sense to Henry. Who wouldn't want that kind of relationship? "Doesn't everyone want an easy relationship?" he asked.

Aunt Kathy smiled at him. "Yes, of course. But some people think being with one person isn't as fun as dating a lot of people. Let's hope Emmett Trask isn't like that." She pulled the car into the garage and turned off the engine, grabbing her bag and leading the way into the kitchen. "Now, let's check in with your parents."

Their mother and father were having a wonderful time in Santa Fe without the rest of the family, which Henry found slightly galling. In fact, they were sitting in the sunny courtyard of a noisy restaurant and couldn't hear too well, but they promised to call back later that night.

"More fun than if we were there?" Henry asked his mother, when it was his turn to talk.

"Of course not, sweetheart," she said diplomatically, "just a different kind of fun. I can't wait to tell you all about it. Everything's going okay with Aunt Kathy? I can't believe she's been there only a day and already has a date! Who is he, anyway? Emmett somebody? She says you boys know him?"

Henry gulped, realizing that they'd never told their mother about their first trip to Emmett's house. "Um, yeah. Emmett Trask. We met him at the library. He's a geologist." All of that was true, at least.

Fortunately, Mrs. Barker was clearly distracted by the bustle at the restaurant and not inclined to ask any more questions. "You make sure you have her cell phone number if she goes out, okay, Hen?"

"We will," Henry promised. Their parents seemed surprisingly amenable to the idea of the boys being left on their own on Sunday afternoon—so amenable that Henry thought they must have misunderstood. But according to Aunt Kathy, it was fine as long as (1) they could reach

Aunt Kathy on her cell phone, (2) it was only for a few hours, and (3) she was home before dark.

Henry, Simon, Jack, and Delilah left Aunt Kathy giddy with excitement about her date. Delilah scooped up Josie, who was circling her legs obligingly, and they all retreated to Henry's bedroom, closing the door behind them. Simon took the note out of his pocket and flattened it on the carpet where they could look at it.

"What was in the saddlebag doesn't belong to you," he read. Josie immediately pounced on it, batting it with one paw. "She loves paper," Henry explained to Delilah, snatching it away from her.

"Well, what was in the saddlebag doesn't belong to *them* either," Jack said staunchly. "Everybody it belonged to is dead."

"But who wrote that?" Delilah demanded, scratching Josie's ears. "And then put it in the basket of my bike? Nobody knew about the map or the coins but us. It's freaky. Not to mention annoying. I don't like people touching my things."

"Well," Simon reasoned, "it doesn't say they know *what* was in the saddlebag."

"No," Henry allowed. "But it sounds like they've figured out that it was something important."

"*We* don't even know whether it's something important," Simon contradicted. "I mean, sure, it's a map. But it's not like we can find the gold mine marked on it. And the coins are not that valuable. They're like the ones in Uncle Hank's coin box in the basement, just old Spanish silver pieces. Remember when we looked them up on the computer? They weren't worth that much."

"Somebody saw us take something out of the saddlebag," Delilah said to Henry. "The only person that could have been is . . ."

Henry nodded grimly. "I know. The person who was shooting at us."

"Maybe they were shooting at us because we found something valuable," Delilah said, running her hand thoughtfully over Josie's sleek back. "Or because we were close to finding something valuable. Not just because we were in the canyon. But still—who could it be?"

Just then, Josie launched herself from Delilah's lap onto Henry's nightstand, knocking over the stack of books there. As the books cascaded to the carpet, *Missing on Superstition Mountain*, the historical society's booklet of strange events and disappearances that Henry had kept carefully tucked under his pile of books, fluttered loose. It landed on Henry's lap.

"Josie!" Henry protested. He picked up the booklet, which he hadn't really looked at since their trip up the mountain to retrieve the three skulls. He absently flipped through to the end, and then gasped.

"What's the matter?" Delilah asked.

Henry folded open the last page and held it for the others to see. A list of historical society members filled the page in a neatly centered column. Under *Emmett Trask, President,* was a list of three officers:

Julia Thomas, Vice President
David Myers, Treasurer
Richard Delgado, Secretary

"Look!" Henry whispered urgently. "Emmett told us that Julia Thomas was the new president of the historical society, but do you see who else is in it? Not just in it, but in charge of it!"

"Myers," Simon said slowly. "The policeman. So that *is* how Mrs. Thomas knew what happened to us on the mountain. And Delgado . . ."

"Sara Delgado," Delilah interjected. "From the cemetery."

Emmett had told them the story of how Sara had

been lost on the mountain for days and had returned in a fugue state, crazed with fear, unable to say what had happened to her. On their first trip to the cemetery, they had had an unsettling conversation with her that didn't make any sense.

"That weird girl!" Jack exclaimed.

"This must be her father," Henry said. "It's like a secret club." He glanced over at Josie, who was watching them impassively from the bed, the scattered pile of books on the carpet below her. Sometimes it almost seemed as if she *meant* to show them things. He thought of her lying on top of the tombstone that said BARKER at the cemetery or waiting in Delilah's yard by the displaced bike.

Simon sat back, running his hand through his hair till it stood in a spiky halo. "So these are the treasure hunters," he said.

"And maybe they're the ones who have been following us and shooting at us and leaving strange notes, trying to stop us from finding the gold," Henry finished for him.

"Well, this only proves that they're in the historical society together," Simon amended. "And they know each other. But if they are the ones following us, they must really believe there *is* gold." He paused, mulling this over. "Let's look at the map again. See if you notice anything new, after what Emmett talked about."

Henry dug through the clutter of shoes and board games on the floor of his closet and pulled out Delilah's pink backpack. He unzipped the side pocket and carefully removed the thick square of brown paper, unfolding it in front of them.

They all leaned over the map, peering at its dark markings: the upside down *V*'s of the mountains, the squiggly line of the creek, the narrow, jagged channels that appeared to indicate canyons.

"This big point on the side has got to be Weaver's Needle," Simon said.

"And here's the little secret canyon," Henry added, tracing it with his index finger. "But I don't see anything that looks like a gold mine, do you?"

"No." Simon shook his head in disappointment. "There was nothing else in that bag with the coins?"

Delilah fished around in the other pocket of the backpack and removed the leather bag of coins. She dumped it out next to the map, and they caught their breath as the shining nugget of gold tumbled onto the carpet. It clinked onto the little pile of coins, flashing in the sunlight. Henry thought about what Emmett had said about its purity; how gold was only attracted to gold, not other elements.

"This gold came from somewhere," Simon said softly, holding the nugget up to the window. The dark bluffs of Superstition Mountain hovered behind it. "We just have to figure out where." He glanced again at the map. "The Lost Dutchman's Mine has to be there . . . it has to."

Delilah ran her fingers over the coins, spreading them across the carpet. "You're sure about these? There's nothing special about them?"

Henry shrugged. "They look the same as the ones in Uncle Hank's coin box."

"But did you ever actually compare them?" Delilah asked.

"No. . . ."

"Well, let's do that," Simon decided, nodding at Delilah. "That's a good idea. Maybe there's something different about them that will be a clue to the location of the gold mine."

They carefully returned the nugget to the pouch, and the pouch and the map to the backpack. For good measure, Simon tucked the threatening note in the pouch too, since they certainly didn't want their mother coming across that in one of her cleaning sprees. Henry scooped up the handful of coins and was just hiding the backpack in the jumble on the floor of his closet when they heard footsteps in the hallway and a knock. Simon swiftly slid the closet door closed just as Aunt Kathy leaned into the bedroom doorway.

"What are you guys doing in here?" she asked. "You're so quiet."

There was a glitch of hesitation, but it was so brief, they hoped she hadn't noticed. At that exact moment, Josie leapt from the bed and shot past her down the hallway, causing her to jump with surprise.

"We were looking at some old coins," Simon said, taking them from Henry and cupping them in his palm. "They're Spanish. Uncle Hank collected them."

Aunt Kathy reached out with one manicured hand and pinched a coin between her thumb and forefinger. "Wow, these are old!" she said. "I wonder where he got them. Did you check to see if they're worth anything?"

Simon nodded. "We looked them up on the computer— even in good condition, they're only worth around forty dollars each. We thought it would be more."

"Well, they're still interesting." She dropped the coin back in Simon's hand. "And that's quite a lot."

"Yeah," Henry agreed. "We're going to compare them to some of the other ones in Uncle Hank's coin box."

"Okay," Aunt Kathy said breezily, "I'll be checking my e-mail in the study if you need me."

Relieved, they hurried past her into the hall and stampeded down the basement stairs.

"Which drawer was it in again?" Jack demanded, yanking the top drawer of Uncle Hank's rolltop desk open.

"The next one," Henry told him. "At the bottom."

Jack pulled the second drawer open and grabbed the oblong rusty-orange metal box, with its delicate pattern of engravings.

"Here, Jack, let me," Simon ordered, taking hold of one end of the box.

"No, I want to," Jack complained, tugging it toward him.

"You guys—" Henry protested.

"Careful," Delilah warned.

But it was too late. The top part of the box slid in one direction and the bottom in another, coming apart in Jack's hands and scattering coins everywhere.

"Jack! Now look what you've done!" Simon scolded. "You broke it."

"No, I didn't," Jack pleaded, his lower lip quivering.

"Hey," Henry said slowly. He took one of the pieces from Jack. "He didn't break it. It's supposed to come apart like this. Look . . . there's a secret compartment."

He turned the metal trough in his hands to show them. It was a thin, flat drawer that fit smoothly into the bottom of the coin box, virtually undetectable when it was closed.

And there was something inside it.

CHAPTER 19
SIGNS AND SYMBOLS

"I thought the inside of the box didn't seem deep enough when we first found the coins!" Simon exclaimed. "Didn't you, Hen?"

Henry had thought that; he remembered being surprised at how flat it was, but he had never imagined there was a secret compartment in the bottom. "What is it?" he asked as Delilah lifted the piece of paper from the drawer.

"A letter," Delilah said. "Or part of one." She held it out, a torn, yellowed scrap with several lines of ink crossing it.

Henry turned on the lamp. "Can you read what it says?"

She placed it on the top of the desk, scanning it. When she lifted her face, her eyes were wide. "Listen to this. *The canyon entrance is on the eastern wall, behind a group of large . . ."* She squinted at the page. *"Boulders. Two cottonwood trees grow opposite the boulders. The entrance is narrow, no wider than a man's shoulders."*

"That sounds like the secret canyon!" Henry exclaimed. "Remember? There were big boulders in front of it, and the path was so skinny in places, I had to squeeze sideways."

Delilah nodded excitedly. "I know. I think it's the same one."

"Keep reading!" Jack cried, jumping up and down.

Delilah held the paper close to the lamp and peered at the writing. *"Continue toward the . . ."* She paused. *"Horse."*

"Horse?" Simon asked. "Are you sure it's not *house*?"

Henry turned to Simon in bewilderment. A horse or a house? Either one seemed equally unlikely in the barren, rough terrain of Superstition Mountain.

Delilah shook her head. "No, it's *horse* . . . look." She showed him the paper, and continued, *"Until the bent tree threads the needle."*

"What horse?" Jack demanded. "We didn't see any horses up there."

"No, and the paper looks old. If there was a horse

in the canyon when this was written, it would probably be dead by now," Simon said. "It's like this note is in code or something."

"Maybe *toward the horse* means a trail that the Spanish

rode their horses on?" Henry suggested. "I mean, the map was in a saddlebag, and I found bones alongside it that had to have come from a horse or a mule or something."

"Maybe." Simon sounded skeptical. "But from the way you described it, and even from this note, it sounds like the entrance to the canyon is too narrow for a horse to get through."

Henry thought back to that day, squeezing between the rough walls of rock until he was inside the little secret canyon. "Yeah," he said. "A horse wouldn't fit." He hesitated. "But what if there's another way in?"

"Keep reading," Simon urged Delilah.

She shook her head, handing him the yellowed piece of paper. "That's it. It says, *Continue toward the horse until the bent tree threads the needle,* and then it ends with three *V*'s, overlapping."

"Three *V*'s? Do you think those are someone's initials?" Simon asked.

Delilah shrugged. "I don't know. I don't remember reading about anybody on the mountain who had so many *V*'s in his name."

"Hey"—Henry leaned forward—"let me see."

He took the paper from Delilah and squinted at the dark script. His heart quickened in his chest. "Remember that other piece of paper, the one we found in this same box with Uncle Hank's coins?" he asked.

Delilah nodded. "Yes, it was the same message that Adolph Ruth left. Those Latin words—"

"*Veni, vidi, vici,*" Henry said. He could hardly breathe. "*I came, I saw, I conquered.*"

"Three *V*'s!" Simon exclaimed. "Do you know what this means? These must be directions . . . to the gold mine!"

CHAPTER 20
"YOU'RE NOT LEAVING ME BEHIND!"

HENRY FELT A THRILL course through him like an electrical current. Were these really the directions to the Lost Dutchman's Mine? Were they suddenly so close to finding the gold that people had been searching for over the span of two centuries—the gold that had cost so many people their lives?

"That's it! That's where the gold is!" Jack shouted.

"Shhhhhh," Henry, Simon, and Delilah responded, all at once.

"Aunt Kathy will hear you," Henry added. "We have to be quiet."

"It doesn't say anything about gold in the letter," Simon cautioned. "And the directions . . . I mean, unless we can figure out what the horse and the bent tree threading the needle are, it's going to be tough to find anything. Who do you think wrote this? Not Uncle Hank."

Henry shook his head. "It's not his handwriting." He turned the paper over. "It isn't signed."

"But at least we have an idea where to look," Simon continued. "In that secret canyon you found. We have to go back up the mountain."

"Yes!" Jack crowed, in a deafening whisper. "When? When can we go?" He raced toward the stairs.

"Sunday," Simon said. "If we go then, Aunt Kathy will be with Emmett."

"That's a great idea," Jack said.

Henry shivered. Back to the canyon where Delilah had fallen? Where they'd been shot at? One thing was certain: whoever had left that note in the basket of Delilah's bike was watching their every move.

"What do you think?" he asked, turning to her. She was leaning against the desk, eyes downcast.

"I can't go," she said morosely. "How can I climb the mountain with this cast?" She lifted her gaze to Henry's, her look pleading. "Do you think . . . could you maybe wait . . . ?"

"Wait!" Jack protested. "We can't wait!"

Simon shook his head. "If we wait till you get your cast off, that'll be weeks. And our parents will be back, and it will be much harder then." He clapped a hand on

Delilah's shoulder, his voice ingratiating. "I really wish you could come! But we'll just have to go alone this time. Plus, it would be good to leave someone here who knows what we're doing. You know where that little canyon is. If something happens and we don't come back, you'll be the perfect person to get help."

"That's true," Henry said, trying to reassure her. "If we run into trouble, you'll be *invaluable*." Silently, he corrected himself. It wasn't *if we run into trouble*; it was *when*.

Abruptly, Delilah straightened. She tossed her braid over her shoulder, eyes blazing. "I can't believe you guys!" she fumed. "You wouldn't even have found that secret canyon except for *me*!"

"How do you figure?" Simon demanded, incredulous. "We were the ones who found the skulls on the cliff. You wouldn't have known anything about the mountain or the canyon except for *us*."

"Yeah!" Jack echoed. "You didn't do anything but break your leg!"

"Exactly," Delilah snapped at him. "And if I hadn't broken my leg, Henry wouldn't have had any reason to go to the bottom of the canyon. And he wouldn't have found the saddlebag or the map or the gold."

Henry's eyes widened. Now she was taking credit for all of that? The gold too? "Hey—" he started to protest, but Delilah stormed on.

"If it wasn't for me, none of you would know anything about that secret canyon which—*hello*—may be the real, actual, exact place to find the Lost Dutchman's Mine— that people have been looking for since the 1800s!"

She crossed her arms and glared at them. Henry had never seen her so mad, not even when they first met her and had tried to take Josie back.

"You already went to the ghost town alone," she said. "You are not going up the mountain without me. And that's final."

"Whoa," Simon said. Even he seemed intimidated by her outburst. "Delilah, calm down. Just think about it for a minute, okay? We can't wait till your cast is off. It's too long. And this Sunday is the perfect opportunity! Our parents are gone, and Aunt Kathy is busy. We know how to get to the canyon now, so it won't take as long as it did before. We know what supplies to bring. It really would be great to have you stay here in case—"

"No! You're not leaving me behind! Not while you do all the fun stuff. It's not fair." Delilah continued to frown at them.

Henry looked from Delilah to Simon. "Why can't she come with us, even with the cast?" he asked tentatively. "It's not like we're riding our bikes. We're just walking anyway . . . and it's supposed to be a walking cast."

Delilah glanced doubtfully at her cast. "I've never climbed rocks in it. I don't think it's meant for that."

"She'll slow us down," Simon said. Delilah's mouth clamped in a hard, mad line, but he continued, "How would she get down into the canyon? She'll fall again."

"Stop talking about me like I'm not here," Delilah said.

"Listen," Simon said to her in a more conciliatory tone. "I wish you could come with us. I really do. But it's too hard for you to climb with your leg like that, and it doesn't make sense for us to wait."

Delilah looked at him in silence for a minute. Then she uncrossed her arms and said coolly, "If you go without me, I'll tell my mom. And she'll call the police. You won't even get halfway to the mountain."

Jack lunged at her. "You are nothing but a big lousy TATTLETALE!" he yelled, raising his fist to pummel her.

"She's worse than that—she's a baby," Simon snapped.

"Wait," Henry said, grabbing Jack around the waist

and struggling to hold him back. "You don't mean that," he said to Delilah. "You wouldn't really tell on us."

"You're not leaving me behind," she repeated stubbornly.

Simon sighed and slumped to the floor, clapping his hands on either side of his head.

"Okay, okay," he said finally. "We don't have a choice. But we are going up the mountain on Sunday, and you'll just have to keep up." He glared back at Delilah. "And when we get to the canyon, I'm not helping you! You'll have to figure out how to climb down on your own."

"Yeah," Jack echoed, glowering at her.

"Don't worry. I will," Delilah retorted.

Henry gulped. He thought of the trek up the mountain, with its rough ground and sharp rocks and sudden, surprising crevices. Arduous as the trip was, it seemed like it was about to become even more difficult.

CHAPTER 21
RETURN TO SUPERSTITION MOUNTAIN

SUNDAY COULDN'T COME soon enough. The boys spent Saturday surreptitiously amassing the supplies they would need to ascend the mountain and search for the gold mine. They assembled their stash in a cardboard moving box in a corner of the garage, on the theory that it was the one area of the house least likely to attract Aunt Kathy's attention. The box filled up slowly over the course of the day. Henry and Simon both watched in growing satisfaction, though Henry's was tinged with worry and Simon's with impatience. Jack, meanwhile, raced around making suggestions and signaling his approval in loud whispers.

What supplies were essential? First: two flashlights. Even though they would make the climb up and back during the day, if they were able to find the mine, it would no doubt be below ground in the dark. Next: a small garden shovel. They debated bringing an actual shovel, but the one in the garage was so heavy and ungainly, they couldn't imagine making the long, hot trip up the mountain carrying it. Finally: a rope, which was hardest to come by—all Simon could find in the shadowy corners of the garage was an old clothesline. But Delilah, who seemed eager to make amends and prove her worth after her outburst, insisted on contributing two jump ropes. She also brought a canvas bag filled with bottles of water and an array of snacks—granola bars, potato chips, chocolate bars, a few apples.

"Did you remember candy?" Jack wanted to know.

"Chocolate," Delilah said, showing him. "Isn't that enough?"

Looking skeptical, Jack retreated to the kitchen for fortifications. "I'm bringing my hunting net too," he announced when he returned, holding their mother's reusable net shopping bag in one hand.

"What for?" Simon demanded. "We're not going to catch anything. It's not that kind of trip."

"Well, we might," Jack said stoutly, adding the net bag and a fistful of candy to the box.

It seemed that everything would fit in two backpacks, so they emptied Simon's large black one and retrieved

Delilah's pink one from Henry's closet. Henry carefully stuffed the pouch with the coins and the nugget into the toe of one of his shoes and shoved it back in the closet. The map they would bring with them, along with the directions from the coin box. Both were quickly sequestered in the outside pocket of Delilah's backpack.

On Sunday, Aunt Kathy was expecting Emmett around twelve o'clock. As Henry lay on his stomach across his parents' bed, she fussed happily in front of the mirror, applying and reapplying her makeup to achieve the perfect "natural" look.

"If you want to look natural, why don't you just not wear makeup?" Henry suggested. He was watching her smooth a creamy beige liquid over her cheeks and throat.

"Oh, no, no, no." Aunt Kathy recoiled in horror. "If I didn't wear makeup, I would just look drab and forgettable. The point of the makeup is to look natural in a better-than-normal way." She turned to face Henry. "There. What do you think?"

Henry had to admit she looked really good, but not like she was covered in makeup. "You look pretty," he said.

"Aw, thanks, honey. Now, if only I could wear my cute sandals. But if we're going to be walking around the countryside, it'll have to be these." Sighing, Aunt Kathy pulled a pair of sneakers out of her suitcase. "Okay, last thing . . ." She gathered her wavy hair into a ponytail. "Up or down?" she asked Henry.

"It looks better down," Henry said. "But you might get all sweaty."

"Good point." Aunt Kathy studied her reflection in the mirror. "I'll wear it down but bring the elastic with me," she decided. "So I can put it up later, if we're hiking and it gets too hot."

"Aunt Kathy, Emmett's here." Simon's voice drifted down the hallway.

"Oh, my goodness, he's right on time," she exclaimed. "Well, I guess this will have to do. Can't keep them waiting on the first date! You have to create the illusion that you're as punctual as they are." She winked at Henry, snatched her purse from the bed, and hurried out of the bedroom.

Henry rolled his eyes and followed her. Emmett was standing awkwardly in the kitchen. Simon and Jack, after announcing his arrival, must have disappeared. "Hey," he said, grinning. "Ready to go? Hi, Henry."

"All set," Aunt Kathy answered merrily. "You're so nice to do this! I can't wait to see the desert and those rocky places you were talking about."

"Sure. It'll be fun." Emmett glanced at her shoes. "Uh . . . do you have hiking boots?"

Aunt Kathy shook her head. "Just my running shoes. But they'll be okay, won't they? They have a grippy bottom." She touched the edge of the kitchen counter for balance and lifted one foot to display the patterned rubber sole.

"Well, we won't go anywhere too rough," Emmett said. "They'll be fine for walking around the desert."

"And we'll be back by five o'clock?" Aunt Kathy asked. "I promised my sister. She was fine with Simon being in charge for the afternoon, but I told her I'd be home before dinner."

"Of course," Emmett said. "That's no problem."

"Simon! Jack! Come say good-bye," Aunt Kathy called.

Simon and Jack came charging in from the garage, with Delilah close on her heels.

"Oh, Delilah! How are you, honey?" Aunt Kathy hesitated. "Emmett and I are just leaving—is it okay with your mom if you're here without a grown-up? Should you call and ask?"

"It's fine," Delilah said easily. "She knows."

"Oh . . . okay, well . . ." Aunt Kathy turned to the boys. "You three—four!—be good while I'm gone. You have my cell number." Aunt Kathy indicated the notepad on the kitchen counter. "I'll call to check in."

"You don't need to do that," Simon said smoothly. "We'll be fine. We might go over to Delilah's."

"Ready?" Emmett held the door for her.

"Yes! I think that's everything," Aunt Kathy said. "Okay, guys, I'll see you around four or five."

With a wide smile and a breezy wave, she followed Emmett out the front door, closing it with finality behind them.

Simon, Henry, Jack, and Delilah stood in the middle of the abruptly silent house, looking at each other.

"Okay," Simon said. "Let's go. We don't have much time."

They hurried to the garage and dug the supplies out of the box, quickly filling the two backpacks. Henry remembered the tube of sun lotion in the kitchen drawer and they covered themselves in it, barely pausing to rub it in.

"Are you sure that's everything?" Delilah asked as she zipped the backpacks. "Map, directions, shovel, flashlights, rope, water, snacks," she rattled off under her breath.

"Candy," Jack added.

"It's everything," Simon said. "Come on."

Just as Simon took his own backpack and Henry pulled Delilah's pink one over his shoulders, they heard a jangle of keys and the creak of the front door swinging open. They all froze. Henry's heart leapt in his chest. Now what?

"Kids?" Aunt Kathy called from the foyer.

"What's she doing back here?" Simon hissed. In one seamless motion, he snatched the pink backpack from Henry and slid his arm out of his own, shoving them both under the kitchen table, seconds before Aunt Kathy bustled into the kitchen. They stood still as statues, even Jack. Henry tried desperately to look blasé.

"Hey," Simon said. "What's the matter?"

Aunt Kathy scanned the kitchen. "Forgot my sunglasses," she said. "Here they are!" She grabbed them from the counter, then paused, surveying the circle of alert faces. "Look at all of you, right where I left you. I hope you're not going to spend the day like this! Why don't you go outside?"

"We will," Simon assured her. "That's what we were just about to do."

"Good! Don't forget to rub in that sun lotion!" Sliding the sunglasses on top of her head, she dashed out the front door as quickly as she'd come.

"Phew." Simon exhaled. "That was close."

"No kidding! I thought she snuck back to check on us," Henry exclaimed.

"She's too busy thinking about Emmett," Delilah said. "She wouldn't even have noticed the backpacks."

"Maybe not," Simon said, "but we couldn't take any chances. Okay, let's go!"

They all ran onto the back deck, Delilah thumping behind with her cast. Josie, who was lying on the top step in a patch of sun, leapt to her feet in annoyance at the commotion. She darted over to the swing set and hid under the slide. There, in its shadows, she watched them cross the yard, the tip of her tail twitching.

"Should we put her in the house so she doesn't follow us?" Henry wondered.

"Nah," Simon said. "She always does what she wants anyway."

They passed through the sparse scrim of trees at the back of the yard and started into the sandy foothills. The giant saguaro cactuses sprung up all around, prickly arms raised—for all the world like guardsmen lifting their hands to warn: "Stop! Go back!" *Go back while you still can,* Henry thought grimly.

Simon paused and turned around, surveying the

perimeter of the neighborhood, the crude line where the scrubby yards ended in desert. "Make sure we're not being followed," he said to Henry, his voice low. "We have to keep checking on that."

Henry glanced nervously over his shoulder. "Okay," he mumbled. Privately, he was wondering what they would possibly do if they found out they *were* being followed. Especially if they were being followed by those members of the historical society—somebody with a gun, like Officer Myers. He shivered, remembering the loud crack of the gunshot in the canyon, shattering the silence. Was this how Uncle Hank had felt, when he fled the irate, gun-wielding frontiersmen he had beaten at poker, and sought refuge in the mountain's rocky nooks and crannies?

What does it matter? Henry thought. They were on their way now, stumbling through the low bushes and across the dry ground, passing the remnants of the sticks Simon had planted weeks ago to mark their way. There was danger ahead and behind them. The only true choice was the choice for adventure. Their path led directly toward the dark, looming shape of Superstition Mountain . . . home of the Thunder God.

CHAPTER 22
THE SOUNDS OF SILENCE

THE CLIMB UP the mountain took less time than before, even with Delilah's slower pace. Henry wasn't sure why . . . was it because the landscape was more familiar this time? The steepness of the path, the pockets of gray-green shade trees, the craggy reddish-brown walls of rock that rose all around them—all of these were recognizable from their earlier treks up the mountain, and yet there was nothing calming about the familiarity. If anything, Henry felt a thin blade of anticipation slicing through him. The cloudless blue sky stretched innocently overhead, but the strange sense of menace prevailed. He remembered what Emmett had said about the Thunder God. He wondered if that was why it always felt like something was watching them. Despite their noisy progress (Jack in the lead, crashing through brush and scattering stones;

Delilah far behind, clomping and thudding up the trail), the mountain seemed eerily quiet. As if it were paying attention.

"How are you doing?" Henry asked Delilah, stopping to rest against a large boulder.

"Okay." She was breathing heavily, and her face was damp with sweat. The sun was beating down, pulsing against their backs. The air was thick with heat. Henry scanned the trail down the mountainside. At first, he and Simon had been checking regularly to make sure nobody was following them. But once the trail became steeper and crowded with rocks, it had taken all of Henry's concentration to keep climbing.

"Does your leg hurt?" he asked Delilah.

"No." She shook her head quickly. Her cast was so covered with brown dust that it was impossible to read the colorful signatures. Henry wondered what her mother would think.

He glanced up the trail to where Simon and Jack were forging ahead, their bright T-shirts bobbing through the wilderness. "Should we slow down?" he asked.

"No!" Delilah pushed determinedly past him.

"Wait," Henry said. "Don't you want some water? It's okay, we can take a break."

She hesitated, panting, and wiped her sleeve across her forehead. She looked so hot and tired that for a minute, Henry was worried she might start to cry. But then he remembered that she hadn't even cried in the canyon when she broke her leg.

He unzipped the backpack and took out a bottle of water, unscrewing the cap for her.

"What's going on?" Simon yelled. "Why'd you stop?"

"I'm thirsty," Henry yelled back. He waved the water bottle. "Want some?"

Simon considered. "Okay. But make it a short break. We don't have much time." As he and Jack headed back down the trail, Henry whispered to Delilah, "Don't worry about Simon. He won't really leave you behind. He just said that to scare you."

Delilah took a long gulp of water and handed the bottle back to him. "I know," she said. "It's like when my mom gets mad 'cuz I'm not ready and says she's going to leave without me." She wiped her face again on her shirt, then smiled at Henry.

Simon and Jack thundered down the path toward them, kicking up clouds of dust. A lizard darted out of the shrubbery. At the sight of them, it panicked and disappeared again.

Taking the water, Simon dumped a little over the top of his head, letting it run down his cheeks. "Man, it's hot," he said.

"Can I have something to eat?" Jack asked.

Simon shook his head. "You have to wait. We don't have time now."

Jack frowned. "You are not the boss of me."

Henry intervened. "We can have a snack when we reach the canyon, Jack. It'll be our reward for getting there."

Jack seemed to accept this logic. "Okay."

And so they climbed on. Henry listened for the stillness in the air, the strange, breathing silence. He imagined the Thunder God guarding the mountain's secrets. How had Uncle Hank survived so many trips up the mountain? Was it because he was an explorer, a bona fide U.S. Army scout? He had been looking for the gold too, hadn't he? Henry thought of his big blue book of Greek myths, the stories of people making offerings to angry gods, to appease them . . . was that what the Thunder God wanted? A sacrifice? Sometimes what the gods wanted was a *human* sacrifice. He remembered Sara Delgado, the daughter of the caretaker at the cemetery, who'd spent days wandering on Superstition Mountain and came back wild-eyed, talking nonsense. Had the Thunder God taken her spirit as an offering?

"Does this seem like the right way?" Delilah asked, looking around.

Simon nodded with conviction. "You haven't been up here as many times as we have. See that stick? That's from our first trip up, when we were chasing Josie."

"Yeah," Jack bragged. "Before you'd ever even heard of the mountain!" He skipped and scrambled ahead, charging over the rocks in the path.

"I may not have been up here as many times as you have, but I've *stayed* up here longer," Delilah pointed out. "Hours and hours. Right, Henry? By ourselves."

"Right," Henry said. *By ourselves except for whoever was shooting at us*, he thought. But she was smiling at him conspiratorially, so he couldn't help but agree.

"Do you think it really was those people from the historical society who shot at us?" Delilah asked. "Mrs. Thomas, Officer Myers, Sara Delgado's father? I mean, if they were trying to kill us, that would make them murderers. Would they do that just to keep us from reaching the gold?"

"I don't know," Henry said grimly, looking behind him. They followed a curve in the path, and suddenly

Weaver's Needle appeared before them, its sharp pinnacle rising boldly from the maze of canyons and bluffs. It pierced the blue sky.

"We're getting close now," Simon urged. "Let's pick up the pace." He started to walk faster, then glanced back at Delilah. Though he said nothing, Henry noticed that Simon deliberately slowed down. Delilah took a deep breath and gamely stomped after him.

"Hurry!" Jack shouted. "I'm hungry!"

"You take the backpack for a while," Simon told him, sliding it off his shoulders and handing it to Jack.

"But—" Jack started to complain. At Simon's look, he changed his mind and snatched it, barreling ahead, his sneakers churning up the dry ground. They were walking several paces behind him when Simon stopped suddenly.

"What's the matter?" Henry asked.

Then he heard it—a dry, raspy, shaking noise, like nuts or seeds rattling in a jar.

What was that?

Simon was standing as still as a statue in the middle of the path. He turned toward Henry very slowly and shook his head imperceptibly. His face was frozen in fear.

There on the side of the path, half hidden by a ledge of rock, was a rattlesnake.

CHAPTER 23
DON'T MOVE

THE SNAKE'S PATTERNED SKIN blended perfectly with the sandy ground. Its triangular head was raised and drawn back over the dense coil of its body, thin tongue flicking.

Henry stopped in his tracks and motioned to Delilah, but she'd already come to an abrupt halt, staring at the snake.

Simon whispered, "What should I do?"

Very quietly, Delilah answered, "Don't move."

Henry nodded. The snake was less than two feet from Simon's legs. Simon wouldn't be able to leap or run to safety before it struck, and its body was as tensed as a spring. It would easily cross the distance between them.

The rattlesnake shook its tail a second time; the same terrifying dry rattle. Henry could see the glint of its small, bright eyes.

They all stood just as they were for what seemed like endless minutes.

Henry's mind was racing. He thought of Uncle Hank, trekking up and down Superstition Mountain dozens of times. He must have run into more than a few rattlesnakes. What would he do?

And what if Simon got bitten? They wouldn't be able to get him down the mountain in time to save him. Henry had read in Jack's book that it didn't work to suck out the poison, like people did in old movies. You shouldn't even move somebody after a snakebite. The important thing was to keep the person quiet so the blood didn't circulate any faster than necessary, to prevent the venom from spreading through his body.

Then they heard Jack's sneakers pounding back down the trail toward them.

"Where *are* you guys?" he yelled.

Henry's heart seized. If Jack stormed into this scene, the snake would surely strike. He forced himself to speak slowly and clearly.

"Stop, Jack. Don't come any closer."

Amazingly, Jack listened. He skidded to a halt several yards from Simon and stared at all of them in bewilderment. Henry realized how strange they must look to him: all of them as still as statues in a garden.

"Snake," Delilah said softly.

"Snake," Jack echoed, staring.

The snake remained poised, a question mark in the air.

"Stay still," Delilah whispered.

Henry thought of *Harry Potter and the Sorcerer's Stone* and the scene where Harry first realizes he can talk to snakes. He stared at the rattlesnake, thinking hard, chanting over and over in his mind, "Don't bite Simon. Don't bite Simon."

"Hold on," Jack whispered to Simon.

"What are you doing?" Henry asked, alarmed.

Henry had never seen Jack move so slowly and carefully in his life. It was like the time-lapse photography in one of those nature films. He took Simon's backpack from his shoulder and unzipped it, pulling their mother's green net shopping bag from inside.

"I can throw the net on it," he said.

"No," Simon said, "it'll strike—"

But before they could stop him, Jack tossed the net through the air.

Henry's eyes widened in horror.

"Jack, stop—"

But to his amazement, the green net landed squarely on top of the snake. Immediately, it started writhing and squirming, but it was caught.

"Quick," Delilah said. "Move out of the way, Simon."

Holding their breath and giving the tangled snake wide berth, they ran past it up the trail.

A minute later, they were out of danger. Simon didn't say anything, but Henry could see that his legs were trembling. He walked a few more yards up the path before collapsing on a rock.

Delilah let out a long breath of relief.

Henry's head was pounding from concentrating so hard. He vaguely remembered some old saying about rattlesnakes . . . how did it go again? *The first person wakes him, the second one makes him mad, and the third one gets bitten.*

"Wow!" Jack crowed. "A real live rattlesnake! Aren't you glad I brought my net?"

Henry thought again how Jack's impulsiveness was sometimes such a virtue. Instead of endlessly agonizing over what action to take, he just DID something . . . and there were times when doing *some*thing was more important than doing the right thing.

Simon shook his head. "That was too dangerous! What if you'd missed? The snake would have bitten me."

"I didn't miss," Jack said. "I saved you! Between my rope in the ghost town and my net up here, I've saved you TWICE. And we got to see a rattlesnake!"

"I wonder how it will get out of the net," Delilah said, her brow furrowing. "I hate to leave it there like that."

Simon looked incredulous. "It almost bit me!"

"I know, but that's not its fault. That's just what snakes do," Delilah countered.

"Oh, it can get out of there," Jack said confidently. "Rattlesnakes are tricky." He proceeded to fire off a volley of facts about rattlesnakes that he'd learned from his library book, including that they could strike at a distance that was two-thirds of their length, that they could smell with their tongues, that they shed their fangs every two months, and that people could die as soon as six hours after a bite.

"Really? Six hours?" Delilah said. "That is not very much time to get help if you're out hiking."

"Okay, can we stop talking about this now?" Simon asked, taking the backpack from Jack and pushing past him into the lead.

"Why?" Jack said. "Did you know rattlesnake bites aren't always poisonous? Most of the time they are, but the snake can decide how much poison to put in when it bites. Sometimes they don't put in any."

"Well, I wouldn't want to count on that," Simon said. "We should probably watch out for these piles of rocks along the trail. They're a good hiding place for snakes."

Henry could tell he was annoyed that Jack was the

one spouting off facts for a change. It was the way Henry himself sometimes felt when one of his brothers used an unusual word . . . that they were crowding into his territory, and if they started doing that, what about him would be so special anymore?

"Yeah," Henry agreed, still too shaken up by the encounter to discuss it further.

Soberly and more tentatively now, they continued along the hint of a trail.

"When will we get to the canyon?" Jack complained.

"Soon," Simon told him. "Soon."

CHAPTER 24
INTO THE CANYON

FINALLY, THEY REACHED the woods. It was cooler here, with the trees shading the rocky path. Through their sparse branches, Henry could see the sun high in the sky. The silence seemed heavier now, the mountain a place resistant to ordinary sounds. He glanced over his shoulder. Still no sign of anyone following them, thank goodness, but there was always the strange shivery feeling of being watched.

"We're getting close now," Simon cried, jubilant. "Come on, pick up the pace." He hesitated, flashing a quick look at Delilah. But she tromped steadily after them, frowning with concentration.

Jack barreled ahead. "Hey!" he yelled moments later. "The CANYON! We're here!"

And there it was. Henry caught his breath as the ground fell away. Suddenly, they were standing on the edge of the steep-walled ravine. The sun glinted off the brown rock. He could see exactly where Delilah had slipped, scraping and bumping all the way down, until she landed in a heap on the canyon floor. And some sixty feet below, there was the pebbly path of the creek bed where he found the saddlebag, and the gray-green shrub where he'd hidden it.

"Look," he said to Delilah, pointing. "That's the bush where I hid the saddlebag, after we took out the map and the pouch of coins . . . and the gold."

She nodded. "I remember." She rubbed her shirt across her forehead, wiping away the sweat and dust. "Hey . . . do you think we'll find my dad's compass?" she asked softly.

Henry scanned the rough slopes. There were so many rocky outcroppings and crevices. It was strange to see the ledge where the skulls had been, empty now. "Maybe," he said doubtfully.

"I really need to find it," Delilah said.

"I know," Henry told her. And he did.

Simon walked along the edge of the cliff, surveying

the canyon wall. Finally, he stopped. "We should go down here. It's not as steep, and there are plenty of places to put your feet."

Then he looked at Delilah's cast. "Are you sure you don't want to wait for us up here?"

She glared at him. "No! I'm coming too. I haven't slowed you down yet."

"The climb up the mountain was nothing compared to this. You already fell once, without a cast."

"You can shut up about that," Delilah grumbled.

"I'm just worried it'll be too hard for you," Simon said, with a more appeasing tone.

"That's for ME to decide," Delilah said. "Not you."

"Okay, okay," Simon said. "Don't get mad." He looked back at the steep wall of the canyon and ran his hand through his hair.

"We'll just have to go down more carefully," Henry said. "You go first and Delilah can follow you."

Simon shook his head. He slipped off his backpack and crouched on the ground, unzipping the main compartment.

"We'll use the jump ropes," he said. "I'll tie them together, then around my waist and Delilah's, in case she loses her balance."

That was a good idea, Henry thought. It would be safer for all of them than if Delilah slipped and knocked into them on the way down.

"I'm not going to lose my—" Delilah began, but Simon cut her off.

"Listen, we're letting you come with us," he said. "I'm not going to get yelled at when you break your other leg. We're doing it this way."

Henry nodded at Delilah. Simon was right. "That's what a real explorer would do," he told her.

Delilah's cheeks reddened, the freckles blazing. "Okay," she said finally.

Simon dug the jump ropes out of the backpack and knotted them securely together. Then he looped the long piece of rope around his waist, tied it tightly, and did the same to Delilah.

Henry peered at the jumble of supplies in the backpack. He saw the metal trough of the little shovel. "Hey," he said. "I can go first and use the shovel to dig footholds for you wherever there isn't a good one." *That* seemed like a real explorer thing to do too; like something Uncle Hank would have thought of.

"That's a great idea, Hen," Simon said enthusiastically. "It'll make it easier for Delilah with the cast."

"I don't need—" she started to protest, but at their combined expressions, she shut up.

"Does that mean I'm last?" Jack demanded. "I want to go first."

"You've been first almost the whole way up the mountain," Simon told him. "That wouldn't be fair. Follow me and put your hands and feet wherever we do."

Jack's lower lip pushed out and he looked crestfallen, which reminded Henry again that he was only six. But it was hard for Jack to disagree with a "fairness" argument, since he relied on those so often himself.

"Come on, Jack," Henry encouraged. "Let's find that gold." He zipped up the black backpack and pulled it over both shoulders. Jack reluctantly took Delilah's pink one, leaving Simon and Delilah free to navigate the canyon wall unencumbered. With the spade in one hand, Henry clambered over the rim of rocks and began to climb down the side of the canyon. The pebbly ground shimmered in the sunlight, far below.

CHAPTER 25

MISSING

WITH HENRY LEADING the way, they descended into the canyon. Henry tucked the spade in the back of his pants, below the backpack, where he could get to it more easily. He lowered himself gingerly over the rough rocks. He would feel blindly with one sneaker till he found a notch or shelf, then step down, gripping the rocks with both hands. Fiercely concentrating on the contours of the canyon wall, he tried not to look beyond the next foothold. The sight of the canyon floor so far below, and the memory of Delilah tumbling down the side, made him sick to his stomach.

"How are you doing?" Simon asked him. "We can go faster if you can."

"Yeah, faster!" Jack echoed.

Delilah, rope tight around her waist, was following

with surprising agility, using her hands to hold her weight and putting her good foot down first, the cast dragging uselessly behind.

"You're pretty good at this," Simon said begrudgingly. "Much better than I expected."

"Well, I'm strong," Delilah said nonchalantly. "I can do pull-ups. When we do the bent-arm hang in gym, I'm always best or second best in the class."

Henry himself was terrible at the bent-arm hang. Of all the goofy exercises and contests that were required in gym class, he considered it the most humiliating.

"I guess you're better with your arms than your legs," he said, looking pointedly at her cast.

But Delilah was unfazed. "No, I'm good with both," she said. "Breaking my leg was just a freak accident. I never broke anything before that."

"Well, you're doing a really good job of climbing down," Simon said. "Henry, you can go faster."

Henry sighed and reapplied himself to the descent. The heat was oppressive. He could feel the mountain's stern judgement gathering around them. Suddenly, he heard a muffled crack and a rumbling noise.

"Look out!" Simon yelled, just as a large boulder above them dislodged and began rolling down the canyon wall.

"Whoa!" Jack cried, shrinking back.

"Stay where you are!" Simon shouted. Delilah cowered.

Henry gripped the side of the canyon and pressed himself flat against it. The large rock tumbled past him, mere feet away, bouncing and rolling to the canyon floor. As suddenly as it had begun, it was over. The thundering crack of it lingered in the air.

"Wow, that was a close one!" Jack cried. "If it had been right above us, it could have knocked us all down—wham! wham! wham! wham!—like dominoes."

Henry secretly wondered if that was exactly what the mountain wanted.

"I wonder why it came loose like that," Delilah said, staring at the area where the rock had come from.

"I bet that happens all the time," Simon said. "Emmett said rock slides are really common."

Henry took a deep breath and squinted up at Simon. "Should we keep going?"

Simon nodded. "Be careful."

So Henry started down again, more wary this time. If he sensed that a foothold wasn't secure, he'd pause from his new position to dig at it with the spade, chipping away and enlarging it. Sometimes the rock was unyielding. Other times, patches of softer rock or dirt gave way, and he succeeded in widening and deepening the hollow.

"Do you see my dad's compass anywhere?" Delilah asked him once.

Henry shook his head. "I think it probably rolled to the bottom, don't you?"

"I guess," she said. "But we didn't see it down there, remember? Keep looking."

"I will," Henry promised.

The sun beat down on him. Whenever he slid the spade back under his waistband, the metal felt cool and sharp against his back.

"Watch out for this one," he'd say sometimes, or "Step over here, it's better."

Delilah climbed steadily after him. Her face was red with exertion, dripping in sweat, but she didn't complain. Suddenly she stopped.

Henry squinted up at her, shielding his eyes from the glare of the sun. "What's the matter?"

"Look," Delilah said. "We're here."

Henry realized he had been so focused on *not* looking down that he'd climbed all the way. They were just a few feet from the canyon floor.

"Hey," he said in wonderment. "We did it."

"Good job," Simon told him, scrambling around Delilah and then helping her to the ground. He quickly untied the rope from their waists and coiled it. Then he took the spade from Henry. Unzipping the backpack, he stuffed them both inside.

"NOW can I have a snack?" Jack asked. "I'm STARVING."

"Sure," Simon said. "But eat quickly."

They rooted through Delilah's backpack and quickly

devoured the apples, one bag of the potato chips, and the granola bars. To Henry, the sharp juiciness of the apples tasted even better than water after the long, hot hike. He rubbed crumbs and juice off his chin and thought of all the books he'd read with starving or thirsty characters who finally found sustenance . . . *My Side of the Mountain, Island of the Blue Dolphins, The Long Winter.*

As they gathered up the wrappers and brushed themselves off, there ensued a vigorous debate over whether to eat the chocolate bars now or wait until after they'd looked for the gold mine. Jack and Delilah wanted candy immediately; Simon argued they should wait.

"We could *compromise*," Henry suggested.

"What's that mean?" Jack asked.

"Find a solution in the middle. Like, we could split one candy bar now and save the rest for later."

"Okay," Jack grumbled, "as long as it means we can eat some candy now."

So they divided up one of the chocolate bars, and Henry had to admit, even the small rectangle of sugary sweetness, soft and sticky from the warm sun, gave him a burst of energy. Jack promptly demanded another chocolate bar, which they divided as before, and then it tasted so good, they all immediately agreed that they had to have one more, at which point Jack began running around like a maniac in a sugar-hyped craze.

"Let's go! Let's go!" he shouted.

"Okay," Simon agreed. "Henry, show us where the secret canyon is. We have to start looking for that gold mine."

"First, let's get the saddlebag," Henry suggested. "Just to see if we missed anything."

He walked past the boulder where Delilah had rested with her broken leg during those hours they were in the canyon alone. He continued in the direction of the secret canyon until he came to the bushes where he'd hidden the saddlebag.

"It's this one, right?" he asked Delilah.

She nodded. "Where the rabbit was."

Henry remembered how a rabbit had shot out from under the bush. When they'd heard the gunshot, that was where he'd tucked the saddlebag. Crouching down, he reached underneath the shrub, pawing at the loose dirt.

Delilah clomped over to him. "Have you got it?"

Henry frowned, still digging with his hand. "I don't feel anything."

"Maybe that's the wrong one," Simon suggested. "There are a lot of little bushes down here."

"Yeah, but I remember where it was," Henry said. "I thought we might need to find it again."

Delilah pursed her lips and gazed down at him, hands on her hips.

"It is definitely that bush. I remember too . . . and look, the dirt is all stirred up around the bottom, like someone's been digging. It's not like that under the other bushes."

Simon bent down with Henry and brushed the pebbly dirt aside.

"You're right," he said slowly. "Somebody must have taken it."

CHAPTER 26
INSIDE THE SECRET CANYON

HENRY TURNED TO DELILAH. "It has to be the person who shot at us! That's the only one who could have seen me hiding it."

"The same person who left the note in my bike basket," Delilah agreed grimly.

"Or people," Simon said.

"Do you think that historical society is a whole gang of . . . *miscreants*?" Henry asked, horrified.

"Who knows," Simon said. "Let's just hope they're not watching us now."

They all simultaneously raised their eyes to the upper cliffs, scanning the broken ridgeline. The blue sky stretched vast and empty overhead. A bird wheeled high above the canyon and disappeared into the trees.

"Nope," Jack declared. "Nobody there."

"Not that we can see, anyway," Henry amended. He continued to watch the woods, thinking about the sharp crack of the gunshot—how unexpected it had been, how it had shattered the air with danger.

Simon roused them. "Okay, you guys. No saddlebag. Let's keep going. Henry, where's the entrance to the little canyon? Do you need the map?"

Henry shook his head. The route was indelibly etched in his mind. He walked swiftly toward the cluster of boulders that nearly blocked the narrow chute.

"Look." Delilah came up behind him, pointing. "The two trees that were in the note. Those must be cottonwoods."

There were two trees growing close to each other, just a few feet from the boulders. "Hey . . . you're right." Henry smiled at her.

Simon and Jack charged up behind them, and together, they peered down the narrow passageway. It was flanked on both sides by steep walls of rock. Henry remembered how he'd explored it the first time, not knowing what lay ahead; there was that thrill of discovering something new, a place no one had been before. Except now it seemed that somebody might have been there before, more than

a hundred years ago . . . if the Lost Dutchman's Mine lay somewhere in the secret canyon.

"This way," Henry told the others. "It's a tight fit."

He slid between the high rock walls, squeezing and bumping his way along the sandy path. Simon followed, then Jack, then Delilah, walking carefully on the uneven ground with her cast.

A few minutes later, the passageway widened, walls slanting away, sky opening up overhead. The secret canyon was much smaller than the other canyon, and utterly silent. Red-brown cliffs rose sharply on either side. A smattering of spindly trees and the same gray-green shrubs grew in the middle. Beyond them, about a hundred yards away, the canyon angled to the right and appeared to end in a wall of rock.

"wow!" Jack yelled, thundering out of the passageway.

"Cool!" Simon said. "You'd never know it was here."

Delilah followed a minute later, stopping to lean against the rocks. They all surveyed the scene.

"It's so quiet," Delilah said. "Even quieter than the rest of the mountain."

It was true, Henry thought. It felt like a place outside of time . . . as if, any minute, dinosaurs could come lumbering around the bend.

Simon dug in the side pocket of Delilah's backpack and took out the map and the note. Gently, he spread them on the canyon floor. "Okay, guys. This is all we have, and there's not much time. Where should we start?"

While Jack raced in circles around them, still energized from the chocolate bars, Henry, Delilah, and Simon scrutinized the note. Henry read it aloud: *"The canyon entrance is on the eastern wall, behind a group of large boulders. Two cottonwood trees grow opposite the boulders. The entrance is narrow, no wider than a man's shoulders. Continue toward the horse until the bent tree threads the needle."* He paused. "And then it ends with the three overlapping *V*'s."

Delilah frowned. "What horse?"

"It can't be a real horse," Simon said. "So what is it?"

Henry scanned the canyon walls, looking for anything that matched the description in the note. *"Continue toward the horse until the bent tree threads the needle,"* he repeated. "So maybe it's something that looks like a h—"

The words died in his mouth.

There, on the right side of the canyon, about sixty yards away, he saw it: a strangely shaped rock, with sharp contours that looked like ears, and a head, and a flowing tail.

In its shadow was a crooked tree.

CHAPTER 27
THREADING THE NEEDLE

"A ROCK HORSE!" Jack yelled. "There!" He pointed in the direction of Henry's gaze.

"It *is* shaped like a horse," Delilah whispered in wonderment. "Look—there's the head."

Henry nodded. It was like a strange, fantastical sculpture, the rough head leaning forward into the canyon, the broad back ending in a windswept tail.

"And that's the bent tree!" Delilah continued. "Do you think that's where the gold mine is?"

"Come on," Simon urged. "Let's find out."

He ran toward the rock horse with Jack close on his heels, dust clouding the air behind them. Henry snatched the map and the note from the canyon floor, then hesitated, waiting for Delilah. Was it possible? Were they really so close to finding the Lost Dutchman's Mine?

"Do you think that could be it?" Delilah asked, awkwardly hustling after Simon and Jack. "I don't get the part about a thread or a needle. And I don't see a hole in the ground, do you?"

When they got to the horse-shaped outcropping, Simon and Jack were climbing all over the boulders that surrounded it.

"What does a gold mine look like?" Jack asked impatiently.

Simon paused. "Emmett said sometimes it can have an entrance, with wooden beams supporting it, almost like a doorway."

Henry tried to remember what else Emmett had told them. "It could just be a hole or a tunnel," he added. "Either way, it'll be close to the ground, won't it?"

"Yeah," Simon said. "Technically. But I don't see anything down there, do you?"

Henry walked along the base of the canyon wall, beneath the rock horse. He saw nothing but ground and rock. He kicked at the loose stones in disappointment.

"The entrance could be hidden," Simon reasoned. "It probably *is* hidden, if nobody has found it after all this time. Maybe we need to look behind some of these boulders."

Handing the map and note to Delilah, Henry joined his brothers, grabbing the top of a big rock and hauling himself up. The edges poked sharply through his sneakers, making it hard to keep his balance. He peered behind the piles of boulders on the ground. He didn't see anything that looked like a tunnel, and most of the rocks were too heavy to move.

Delilah sighed. "It's not here. We must be missing something."

"Read the note again," Henry suggested.

Delilah squinted down at the scrap of paper in her hand, which flashed brightly in the midday sun. *"Continue toward the horse until the bent tree threads the needle."*

"What does that mean? Here's the tree, but where's the thread?" Henry sighed. "I don't get it. Let's look at the map again."

"But we've gone over it so many times," Delilah said. "There were no markings that seemed to be a gold mine."

Nonetheless, she spread the map on a rock and leaned over it, while Henry scrambled down to join her. Together, they stared at the paper, trying to unravel its secrets. Henry's eyes followed the crude line of the main canyon, then the smaller tributary that signified the little canyon. All around these were the upside-down *V*'s,

which seemed to represent the cliffs and crags of the mountains.

"Henry," Delilah said slowly.

"What?"

"Look at this."

"What? The upside down *V*'s? That's the symbol for the mountains."

"No, look closer. These are different from the others." Delilah touched the paper gently with her index finger. "They're right side up. They're actual *V*'s." She raised her eyes slowly to his.

"Yeah . . . so?" Then Henry realized what she meant. In the midst of the upside-down *V*'s that showed the mountains were three that were upright. And they overlapped.

He stared at Delilah, eyes wide.

"*Veni, vidi, vici,*" Delilah whispered. "It must be the symbol for the gold mine!"

Henry grabbed her arm in pure jubilation. "Simon! Jack!" he yelled.

Delilah waved the map above her head. "We found it!"

Simon and Jack came running over the rocks and leapt to the ground.

"Shhh," Simon cautioned, scanning the rim of the canyon. "Don't be so loud. Where? Is there something on the map?"

"Look!" Delilah thrust the map in their faces, while Henry explained, "The overlapping *V*'s! *Veni, vidi, vici*— just like Adolph Ruth's letter, and the little paper we found in Uncle Hank's coinbox, and the initials at the bottom of these directions."

"That must be it!" Simon exclaimed. "So it's not on this side of the canyon at all. It's all the way across, on the other side."

"Where?" Jack bounced on his sneakers. "Where's the gold mine?"

"Exactly opposite where we've been looking," Henry told him, pointing. He surveyed the wall of the canyon facing them, with its rough vertical ridges and the mass of boulders at the base, and began walking toward it.

"But then what's with those directions in the message?" Simon wondered, picking up the slip of paper and reading it to himself. "The rock horse and the bent tree? They're on this side."

Henry stood in the middle of the canyon, turning slowly around, his eyes tracing the rock walls that rose in every direction. Just above the horse-shaped rock, hovering over the bluff, he glimpsed the craggy spire of Weaver's Needle.

Suddenly, he understood.

"The bent tree . . . threading the needle . . . ," he began.

Simon followed his gaze. "Weaver's Needle—that's it! We have to find the place where the view of this tree makes it look like it's threading Weaver's Needle. That's where the gold mine will be!"

Even Delilah was running at this point, stumbling awkwardly over the canyon floor. They reached the other side of the canyon and looked back in the direction of the rock horse and the crooked tree, which rose toward the sky and then abruptly turned, its trunk shooting out parallel to the ground.

Simon dropped to his knees and scrambled along the dusty ground, scrutinizing the twist in the tree's trunk and its alignment with the spire of Weaver's Needle.

"Here!" he said finally. "Look at it now! From this spot right here, the tree looks like it's running through Weaver's Needle and bending at the tip—threading the needle!"

Jack charged over to him. "Then where's the GOLD MINE?"

They all scanned the base of the canyon wall. There were so many boulders strewn along it. Henry couldn't see anything that looked like a tunnel.

"It has to be here," Delilah breathed. "It just has to be."

"Look behind the rocks," Simon directed.

Then Henry saw it. A jagged cleft, almost like a fold, where a wing of rock jutted out parallel to the canyon wall. When Henry faced it, it looked like it *was* the canyon wall, corrugated with cracks and crevices, but when he walked around to the side, he found a hidden passageway, obscured by the curtain of rock. Peering into the fold, he saw that at its base was something that looked like a cave.

CHAPTER 28
INTO THE DARKNESS

HENRY CLIMBED OVER the rocks and into the shadowy corridor. The ground in front of it was worn flat . . . as if someone had gone in and out of the cave many hundreds of times. On the wall above the rocky cavern, he could see a cluster of faded scratches and marks. They were designs, he realized, but they didn't look like anything he'd seen before. There were several humanlike stick figures. Some were upright, while others lay flat, horizontal. They were surrounded by pale circles.

"You guys," he called faintly.

"Where are you, Hen?" Simon called back.

"Here," Henry said, unable to move, unable to breathe.

Simon, Jack, and Delilah crowded at the opening of the passageway, blocking the sunlight. They stared at the dark hole in the wall of rock.

"Oh!" Delilah gasped.

"*Wow,*" Simon breathed.

"The MINE! The Lost Dutchman's MINE!" Jack cried. He raced toward the entrance.

"Keep it down, Jack," Simon warned. "And wait a minute. We need the flashlights, the garden shovel, and the rope. Let me go first."

He took the map from Delilah and carefully returned it, along with the note, to the side pocket of the pink backpack. Then he retrieved the supplies, coiling the knotted jump rope over his shoulder and handing one of the flashlights to Henry.

"Come on, follow me."

Delilah paused at the entrance, lifting her eyes to the pale designs on the rock overhead. "What are those?" she asked.

They all stared at the ancient drawings.

"Probably just Indian art," Simon said. "Petroglyphs. Remember? That's what Emmett was going to show Aunt Kathy today."

Delilah tilted her head, considering the figures. "Why are some of them lying down?" she asked.

Jack pushed past them into the cave. "Maybe they're dead," he offered cheerfully.

Henry shuddered. That was just what he was afraid of. What if these drawings were some kind of warning?

"Hmmm," Delilah said, frowning slightly. She took the garden shovel from Simon and trudged after Jack.

"Come on, Hen," Simon urged.

Henry's heart was pounding so loudly in his chest he could hardly concentrate on anything else. Were they really so close to the gold that had been kept a secret for over a hundred years?

He directed the beam of his flashlight into the dark cave. It was barely tall enough for him to stand up. A grown man wouldn't have been able to—even Simon had to duck his head. The tunnel-like entrance curved into the mountain.

Delilah and Jack were waiting at the edge of the light. It was pitch-black ahead, an impenetrable darkness beyond the arc of the flashlight.

"How far do you think it goes?" Delilah asked.

"I don't know," Simon said quietly. "I guess we'll find out."

Simon led the way, with Delilah following. The air temperature had dropped several degrees, and Henry felt the skin on his arms prickle with the chill. The cave's silence fell over them like a blanket. They filed through the tunnel, aware of every scuff and scrape of their feet on the cold stone floor.

Jack hung back. "I don't like this," he said.

Henry looked at him in surprise. "How come? It's just a cave. We're exploring!"

"It's all closed in. It's too dark."

"But you're not scared of the dark," Henry said. He had never known Jack to be afraid of anything.

"I'm not scared," Jack said.

"Okay, okay," Henry said. "Then what is it?"

"I don't know."

Henry flashed the light toward him and saw that Jack's lower lip was quivering. His face looked about to crumple.

"Here, do you want to hold the flashlight?" he asked quickly.

Jack shook his head.

"What's going on back there?" Simon's voice echoed thinly through the tunnel. "Where are you guys?"

"Coming," Henry called, trying to think what to say to Jack, who looked as if he was about to turn and run out of the cave.

"It's okay, Jack. We're all together. Know what this is like?"

"What?" Jack mumbled suspiciously.

"Journey to the Center of the Earth," Henry said. "It's a really cool book about explorers who go down into the crater of a volcano, through a tunnel to the center of the earth. They meet prehistoric animals! And discover oceans."

Jack's eyes narrowed, as if he thought he was being duped. "Do you think there are prehistoric animals here?"

"Well, no," Henry admitted. "But there might be gold! Don't you want to try to find it?"

Jack nodded mutely, but still didn't move.

"Come on, Jack. Think of all the things we've done to get here, and you haven't been scared at all. Not once. Starting with falling down into the canyon that first time, when we found the skulls. And then at the cemetery, seeing our own name on a tombstone. And going back up the mountain to get the skulls, and then after Delilah broke her leg, you and Simon had to go down by yourselves in the dark. And the ghost town, Simon crashing through the floor into the cellar with . . . well, whatever that was. You saved him, remember? And today, the rattlesnake." Henry let out a long breath. "This old cave is nothing compared with all of that."

"You did all of those things too," Jack said.

Henry nodded slowly. "Yeah, I did."

"You're a real explorer, Henry." Jack's face, pale in the beam of the flashlight, was full of admiration. "Just like Uncle Hank."

And Henry realized with a kind of wonderment that it was true. Sometimes things turned out just as you planned them—even though you never truly believed they would happen. It had been hard to see it at the time; how each part fit into the whole, how all of the individual adventures combined to create a picture of someone who was exactly as fearless, resourceful, and unflappable as Henry so longed to be. And so what if he'd been afraid? Or filled with doubt? Or had wanted, at different times, to turn back? It didn't matter. In the end, he had done all of it.

He grabbed Jack's arm and said, "Come on. Let's find that gold."

"Hey," Simon called from far ahead, "look."

Henry and Jack hurried to catch up, and suddenly they were standing in a cavern with walls that looked like they had been diligently chipped away to hollow out a larger space. Henry raised his flashlight and shone it on the ceiling.

"I don't see any gold," Jack said. "What if it's just a

cave?" He hesitated. "What if it's a cave with something LIVING in it . . . like a mountain lion?"

"It's not, Jack," Simon said quickly. "Do you see any signs of an animal?"

Jack shook his head, subdued. "But it feels weird in here."

Henry knew what he meant. As quiet as it was, the cave had a feeling of *presence*.

"Hey," Delilah said, "look at this! There's a ladder."

Simon directed his flashlight to where she was pointing, and there, close to the rock wall, was a ragged hole in the floor. The wooden shafts and rungs of a ladder poked out of it.

"It's a good thing you saw that," Henry told her. "We might have fallen in."

"Yeah," Simon agreed. "See, Jack? People have been here! It must be a mine. This ladder will take us down to the next level."

"A mine has levels?" That had never occurred to Henry. How deep into the ground would they have to go?

Simon leaned over the hole and swung his flashlight back and forth, illuminating the ladder. It dropped down about twelve feet. The wood was old and splintered, and it appeared to be missing a couple of rungs.

"Well, this one has at least two levels," Simon said. "Maybe more. Be careful on the ladder. It looks pretty rickety."

He crouched down and started to lower himself onto the ladder when Delilah stopped him.

"I can't do that," she said.

"Sure you can," Simon told her. "You climbed all the way down into the canyon. That was harder than this."

He lifted the beam of his flashlight to Delilah's face. Henry saw that, for the first time all day, it was pinched and pale.

"I know," she said slowly. "But I was tied to you, and I could hold on to the rocks with my hands. I didn't have to put much weight on my cast." Her eyes were fixed on the ladder. She shook her head. "There aren't even enough rungs."

Privately, Henry agreed with her. She could fall or hurt herself, and if she did, how would they ever get her out of here? He thought of how he and Delilah had waited for hours in the canyon when she broke her leg. The idea of being stuck in this black hole of a mine was unbearable to even contemplate.

Simon looked at her, then back at the ladder. "You're right," he said finally. "It isn't safe for you." He hesitated. "And you don't want us to go down without you." He didn't say this with any accusation in his voice, Henry noticed. It was just a statement.

"No," Delilah said. "You should go ahead."

They all stared at her. "We've come too far," she said. "You have to go on and try to find the gold."

"Really?" Jack said in disbelief.

"Are you sure?" Simon stayed where he was, his flashlight trained on her pale face.

Henry looked at her, shivering at the edge of the hole, with her thin arms and mussed-up braid and dirty cast. He understood abruptly how tired she was. The climb had been hard for her. "Do you want me to stay with you?"

Delilah shook her head firmly. "No, you guys should all go. It's just . . ." She hesitated. "I don't want to wait in here by myself." She shivered. "It's kind of cold."

Simon angled the flashlight beam onto his wristwatch. "Listen, it's one thirty. We should leave here in half an hour to make sure we have time to get home before Aunt Kathy and Emmett come back. Henry, walk her back to the entrance so she can wait for us outside. But hurry."

"I could wait with her outside," Jack offered. Simon and Delilah looked at him in shock.

"But, Jack," Henry said gently, "we've come so far."

Jack sighed and nodded resignedly. "Okay."

So Delilah handed the garden shovel to Jack, and Henry took the flashlight and guided her across the cavern and back through the tunnel, where they walked single file to the mine's entrance. The sunlight nearly blinded them, and the air felt warmer immediately.

"Wow, it's so bright," Delilah said, leaning against a rock. "I'll wait right here." She looked up at the petroglyphs and frowned slightly. "Hurry, Henry."

"I will," Henry promised.

He started back into the mine, feeling a strange pang at leaving her and the bright ordinariness of daylight. Holding the flashlight in front of him, he strode into the tunnel, heading straight into the heart of the mountain.

CHAPTER 29
THE DUTCHMAN'S SECRET

WHEN HE REACHED the cavern, Henry found Simon already halfway down the ladder as Jack leaned over the hole, shining the flashlight for him.

"I'm next," Jack said.

"Okay," Henry agreed, "but go slowly. See the gaps in the ladder? You'll have to climb over those parts."

Jack handed the flashlight down to Simon, who kept it trained on the ladder while Henry helped Jack into the hole. Jack gamely heaved himself down the ladder and, a moment later, jumped from a middle rung to the ground.

"Hen, give him your flashlight," Simon said. "It's easier if you use both hands."

Henry tossed down the flashlight, which Jack caught

and immediately started swinging around, sending bright rays of light in every direction.

"Cool!" he cried, sounding more like his old self. "There's stuff down here!"

"What stuff?" Henry asked as he turned around and lowered himself into the hole, feeling for a wooden rung with his foot.

"Look, a bucket! What's this, Simon?"

"Hey, you're right," Simon said. "There are buckets down here . . . and a pickax! We must be in the mine!"

Henry climbed quickly down, stretching his legs over the gaps, the wood rough against his palms. He joined his brothers and squinted into the darkness.

Now they were standing in another chamber of the mine, cooler and vaguely damp. The air smelled pungently of earth.

Two wooden buckets sat a few yards from the ladder. In the faint beam of the flashlight, their handles appeared dark with rust. Henry could see a large pickax leaning against one wall, its curving metal blade covered in dry dirt.

Who left it there? he wondered. *And how long ago?*

"There's another tunnel," Simon said urgently. "We don't have much time. Come on."

Together they started into the narrow passageway, ducking their heads and pushing through its dark contours. The cold, rough walls scraped against Henry's arms.

It was like being inside an animal, he thought, moving through the twisted bowels of a living creature.

Almost immediately, the tunnel opened out again into a new cavern. They stumbled together into the center of it.

"This mine goes on forev—" Simon started to say, but the words caught in his throat.

He lifted his flashlight.

Simultaneously, Henry lifted his.

There, in the arcs of white light, they could see walls of glistening, pearly quartz. And shot through the walls were streaks of lustrous, shining, brilliant . . .

GOLD.

CHAPTER 30

RUN!

"OH, MY GOSH," Simon gasped.

"It's real," Henry whispered.

"We found it!" Jack shouted. "We found the mine!" He whirled in the middle of the cavern, swinging his flashlight wildly at the walls that glittered all around them.

Simon turned to Henry, his eyes huge. "This is it," he said, barely able to speak the words. "The Lost Dutchman's Mine."

"I can't believe we found it," Henry whispered. "After all this time."

He thought of Uncle Hank and his treks up Superstition Mountain, the box with the Spanish coins and the hidden note. How long had he searched for the gold mine? Would they ever know if he made it this far?

If only he were alive to see them now! To see Henry, his namesake, standing in a cavern in the black heart of Superstition Mountain, surrounded by gorgeous, glittering, glistening gold.

"Can we take some?" Jack wanted to know. "How do we get it out of the rock?"

Simon shook his head. "We don't have time, Jack. But now we know where it is!"

"Hey, look!" Jack crowed. "There are little pieces on the ground."

Henry saw that he was right. At the base of the wall with the shining veins of gold, there was a scattering of tiny flakes, the remnants of someone's efforts with a pickax. Jack squatted down to gather a handful of them, stuffing them into his pocket.

Henry and Simon were starting to crouch next to him when Simon turned abruptly, looking back down the tunnel. "What's that?"

They craned into the thick silence, listening. Faint and far away, Henry heard shouts.

"It's Delilah," he said. "She's calling us." He listened again, then stared at Simon. "Something's wrong."

They ran. Back through the tunnel, into the lower

cavern, up the ladder, scrambling and hoisting themselves, juggling the flashlights, the rope, the garden shovel.

"We're coming," Henry yelled, as loud as he could. "What's the matter?"

"Run!" Delilah was shouting. "Get out of there!"

"Why? What is it?" Simon called to her.

Then they heard it. So distant, Henry wasn't sure at first that it was even a sound. It felt like movement, like a shift in the air . . . a building vibration.

"What's that noise?" Jack asked.

"I don't know," Simon said grimly. "Hurry!"

They were running through the upper chamber now, into the tunnel toward the mine's entrance. They could hear it clearly—a distant, growing thunder.

The very ground seemed to tremble beneath their feet.

"Simon!" Henry cried. "Is it . . . the Thunder God?"

Then he saw Delilah at the mouth of the cave, her face white and panicked.

"It's a rock slide," she cried. "We have to get out of here, or we'll be trapped."

Together they fled the cave, snatching up the backpacks and running as fast as they could through the rocky passageway toward the canyon. The noise became deafening.

High overhead, Henry could see part of the cliff breaking away. Rock after giant rock tumbled down the steep slope, crashing into the canyon.

"Don't stop," Simon yelled, yanking Jack out of the passageway and running into the middle of the canyon, away from the bent tree and the rock horse, back toward the place where they'd entered.

Henry grabbed Delilah's hand, pulling her along. "Faster," he urged. "We have to go faster."

It was then that he saw a black streak ahead of them. It darted after Simon and Jack.

Josie!

"Hey! It's Josie!" he yelled to Simon over the crash and shattering of rocks.

"I know. I saw her," Simon called. "Hurry!"

As they rushed into the rocky inlet that had led them to the secret canyon, they paused, just for a moment—all of them clustered on the threshold. They looked back at the fold in the canyon wall that hid the Lost Dutchman's Mine.

The avalanche of rocks poured down all around it

and then over it, rock after rock, thundering into the
narrow corridor. By the time the avalanche stopped, the
entrance to the mine was entirely buried in boulders.

CHAPTER 31
"SOMEBODY'S UP HERE WITH US...."

AS THEY MADE their way into the main canyon, they couldn't stop talking, peppering one another with questions, their words blending and braiding.

"What happened?" Delilah asked. "What did you find in there?"

"Gold!" Jack boomed, while Henry asked in turn, "How did the rock slide start? When did Josie show up?"

"Where?" Delilah cried. "What did it look like? Was it really the mine?"

And then they had to tell her all about the buckets and pickax and tunnel to the lower cavern, with its pale quartz walls streaked with shining veins of gold.

"It was like being inside a treasure chest," Henry told her. He pictured the treasure chest in *Treasure Island*.

"And I took some!" Jack said. "And it's all mine!"

Simon frowned at him. "We should share that. We found it together."

"Nuh-uh." Jack shook his head vigorously. "You should have gotten your own." Then he whirled around, shouting, "I am glad to be out of there! It was too dark and squeezy in that cave."

"Jack, keep it down," Simon scolded. "Do you want the whole world to hear you?"

Henry thought about the cascade of rocks that had descended over the cave, burying it . . . perhaps forever. Had the Thunder God done that? To keep them away from the gold?

"How did the rock slide start?" he asked Delilah again.

She shook her head. "I don't know. I heard a rock fall, like it did when we were climbing down into the canyon, and I thought that was going to be it. But then after a minute, another fell, then another, and then part of the cliff just seemed to break off."

Simon's brow was furrowed. "Did you see anybody up there?"

"Where?" Delilah asked. And then, understanding, "At the top of the cliff? No, nobody. You think . . ." Her voice trailed off, and Henry finished for her, filled with dread. "You think that someone caused the avalanche on purpose? That someone's up here with us?" Nervously, he scanned the ridge, empty against the blue sky.

"I don't know," Simon said. "But we should watch out. And hurry."

"I want to see the gold," Delilah protested.

"When we get home," Simon told her. "It's after two o'clock. We don't have time now."

They hurried through the canyon to the side where they'd climbed down, where the footholds Henry had dug charted a route to the top of the cliff. Simon quickly looped the rope around his waist, then Delilah's, knotting it tightly.

"You go first, Henry. Then I'll come with Delilah. Jack will be last. You guys take the backpacks again."

"What about Josie?" Henry asked. She had raced ahead of them, darting under the gray-green shrubs, looking for rabbits, no doubt.

"She'll be okay," Simon said. "She followed us down here—she can follow us back."

Delilah hesitated, turning to Henry. "What about my dad's compass? I have to look for it. I need it, Henry."

"We have to GO!" Simon snapped. "We can get you another compass."

Henry, seeing her crestfallen face, whispered, "It's

okay. We don't have time now. But we'll be back." He was certain it was true.

So they started up the canyon wall. Even though the route was nearly straight up, it was easier this time, because the footholds marked the way and gave them something to step on.

"When did Josie come?" Henry called down to Delilah.

"It was the strangest thing," she said, breathing heavily as she climbed after Simon. "I was waiting for you guys, just sitting there, and I heard a rustling noise. When I looked, she was coming toward me. She only let me pet her for a minute. Then she darted into the cave, and I thought she was going to find you, but she started playing with something."

"What was it?" Henry asked.

"I don't know," Delilah said. "She was batting at it."

Henry frowned. "I wonder what it could have been."

Delilah shrugged. "Then all of a sudden, she started pacing back and forth. She seemed really nervous or something, and that's when I heard the first rock fall. And then a bunch of rocks were falling, and I started yelling for you."

"It was the Thunder God," Henry said softly.

"It was an avalanche," Simon corrected. "Or maybe it was those people from the historical society," he added quietly.

"It sure sounded like the Thunder God," Delilah said. "I couldn't believe how loud it was."

"You should have gotten out of there," Simon told her. "You could have been buried under all those rocks."

"I know," Delilah said matter-of-factly. "But I wasn't going to leave you guys in the cave."

Thank goodness she had yelled to them when she did, Henry thought. A minute later, and they would never have been able to make it out. He remembered every book and movie he'd ever seen where people were buried alive. Emmett said that had happened to miners on the mountain, and now it had almost happened to them.

Henry gripped a ledge of rock and hauled himself up, concentrating on the slope ahead. The backpack was heavy on his shoulders, and he could feel the afternoon sun burning the back of his neck. He thought of the petroglyph above the entrance to the mine, with the stick figures flat on their backs. It had felt like a warning. Then he thought of the storm of rocks crashing to the ground. Finally, he thought of the Thunder God, willing to do anything to guard the mountain's secrets. Despite the heat, a sharp chill prickled through him.

"Hey," Jack shouted, "Josie's coming."

Henry paused for a minute, wiping sweat from his eyes with one arm. He glanced back over the dizzying void of the canyon. He could see Josie's small black body far below, zigzagging easily up the steep slope.

"Keep going, Hen," Simon told him. "We're almost at the top."

And then they were. They clambered over the rocks until they were standing on flat ground.

They took a quick water break—and water had never tasted so good to Henry, coursing coolly down his parched throat—but they were all too hot and exhausted to be hungry, so they turned their attention to the faint remnants of the path and began their hurried journey home. Henry could feel the mountain watching, pulsing its disapproval all around them.

CHAPTER 32
STONES ON THE PATH

THEY TROMPED DOWN the mountain largely in silence. Delilah looked exhausted, Henry thought. She bumped along on her cast, but she was much slower than she'd been on the way up, and she eventually dropped into last place by a good distance. Henry kept slowing down to check on her.

"Are you okay? Do you want to rest?"

She shook her head, and Simon called from up ahead, "We don't have time. She can rest when we get home."

Home! It had never sounded so wonderful to Henry. Or so far away.

They continued down the uneven trail, marked occasionally by the sticks they had left on their first journey up the mountain. At least it was broad daylight. There was no danger of getting lost in the dark, though the path was narrow in places, and occluded by shrubbery or grass. Sometimes it was hard to know they had gone the right way.

"Is that you guys?" Simon asked.

"What?" Henry called.

Simon was standing still, looking around. "I don't know. I thought I heard something. Shhhhh, be quiet for a minute."

They stood absolutely still, even Jack, listening. The air was hot and motionless. Henry didn't hear anything except their own breathing.

"Is it Josie?" Henry asked.

Simon shook his head. "No. She ran past us a long time ago. She's way ahead now."

Henry peered back up the rocky length of the trail. "What did it sound like?"

A furrow of worry creased Simon's forehead. "Something behind us. In the bushes. It was probably just you guys."

"Do you think someone's following us?" Delilah turned to squint at the winding contours of the trail. The tufts of dry grass alongside it shimmered in the afternoon sun. A gray lizard darted under a shrub. Otherwise, nothing stirred.

"I don't know," Simon repeated. "I don't like hearing things I can't see."

Henry nodded slowly. "Like when you fell into the basement in the ghost town. With whatever was down there."

"Yeah," Simon said. "Like that. Let's keep going."

They began their descent again, but Henry kept glancing back over his shoulder, his neck prickling with fear.

"What time is it?" Jack wanted to know.

Simon extended his wrist, and the face of his watch flashed whitely. "Three thirty. Aunt Kathy might be back as early as four."

"Can't we have a snack?" Jack complained. "I want more candy."

"When we get home," Simon told him. "It will be your reward."

"That's what you always say. I don't want it to be my reward. I want it now. And this is too heavy. I need a rest." Jack shifted Delilah's backpack off his shoulders and dropped it abruptly on the ground, stopping in the middle of the path.

Henry picked it up. "Come on, Jack," he coaxed.

"Remember what we talked about? Do you think this is what real explorers do when they get tired?"

"Yes!" Jack said defiantly.

"Hey," Simon said, "look at that."

He pointed a few yards ahead. On the edge of the trail, Henry saw their mother's green net shopping bag, lying in an empty heap. The rattlesnake was gone.

"Oh, good," Delilah said. "It got free."

"Right," Simon said. "Which means it *is* free. Which means we have to be careful walking through here, 'cuz it could be anywhere."

Henry touched Simon's arm. "What's that?" he asked softly.

"What?" Simon asked. "Do you see the snake?"

"No," Henry said slowly. "Something else."

A short distance past the green bag, smack in the middle of the path, there was a small, neat pile of stones, stacked into a triangular tower.

"Huh," Simon said. "That wasn't there before."

Cautiously, they walked down the trail toward it.

"What *is* that thing?" Jack asked.

"I'm not sure," Simon said. "Somebody made it."

"Simon." Henry froze.

"What is it?"

"Look."

At the base of the pile of stones, something was scratched into the dirt. Thick, crooked letters, dug into the ground with a stick:

STAY AWAY

They all looked at each other.

"Who could have written that?" Delilah asked.

Simon's mouth narrowed to a tense line. "Maybe whoever shot at you in the canyon. Whoever followed us. Whoever tried to bury us in a rock slide! We need to get home NOW."

Henry lingered, his eyes fixed on the dusty message. Was it a message from the mountain itself? A warning from the Thunder God, guarding his gold?

Suddenly, nobody felt like resting anymore. They began to hurry again, bumping and stomping along, stirring up dust in clouds that made them cough and choke. Even Jack no longer complained. They had to get home.

CHAPTER 33
OUT OF DANGER

"THERE IT IS!" Simon cried. They all breathed a sigh of relief. The roof of their house—Uncle Hank's house—rose amidst the tall cactuses.

"Is there a car in the driveway?" Henry asked nervously.

Simon shook his head. "No, we beat them back. It isn't even four yet. But let's go inside and try to clean off." He glanced at Delilah. "You especially."

Henry saw that she was covered in grime, her braid a messy tangle. Her cast had not even one square of white left on it. He wondered if her mother would be angry.

Delilah didn't bother to protest. "I need to call my mom too," she said.

They thudded up the back steps onto the deck. Simon

yanked the sliding door open, and Josie came running from nowhere, streaking past them into the house.

"Josie!" Jack exclaimed. "She beat us down the mountain."

"That's how Josie is," Henry said, smiling, relieved that she too was safely home.

"Hey," said Jack. "Look . . . she has something in her mouth. Maybe she KILLED an animal on the mountain!"

He plopped down on the kitchen floor and grabbed the middle of Josie's body with both hands, hauling her onto his lap. She writhed in irritation.

Delilah turned to Henry. "Maybe it's whatever she was playing with in the cave."

"Before the avalanche started?" Henry asked. "The thing she was batting around?"

"Have a look," Simon ordered. Henry knelt down next to Jack, who was forcefully prying Josie's jaws open. Hissing, ears flat against her head, Josie struck him twice with her paw and shot out of the kitchen.

Jack held a crumpled wad aloft.

"It's just a piece of paper," he complained.

"Really?" Henry asked, taking the damp ball from Jack's outstretched hand. Gently, he unfurled it, smoothing it in his palm.

Then he caught his breath.

"What is it?" Delilah asked, leaning over his shoulder.

Henry held it up for them to see. It was a wrinkled,

cream-colored piece of stationery. The name Henry Cormody was emblazoned in black script across the top. It was the same stationery they'd seen in Uncle Hank's desk in the basement. Beneath the name, in handwriting Henry immediately recognized as Uncle Hank's from various postcards and birthday cards that had arrived over the years, were four sentences now searing in their familiarity:

The canyon entrance is on the eastern wall, behind a group of large boulders. Two cottonwood trees grow opposite the boulders. The entrance is narrow, no wider than a man's shoulders. Continue toward the horse until the bent tree threads the needle.

"The directions to the gold mine!" Simon said. He turned urgently to Delilah. "Where did you say Josie found this?"

"I don't know exactly," Delilah said, shaking her head. "Near the entrance to the cave."

"Do you know what this means?" Simon whirled to Henry, his eyes blazing.

Henry nodded, his heart thudding. "It means Uncle Hank found the mine! He knew where the secret canyon was. He found the gold."

"He did?" Jack bounced to his feet. "But then why wasn't he RICH? How come he didn't bring it all back here?"

They looked at one another in confusion. The Lost Dutchman's Mine was the richest vein of gold in the entire country. If Uncle Hank had found it, why did he keep it a secret?

Delilah shook her head. "Why would he copy the directions like this? Why didn't he just bring the other paper with him, like we did?"

"Probably because he didn't want to lose it. He wanted to keep the original copy safe," Simon said thoughtfully. "We should have done that too, actually."

Henry nodded. "It still doesn't explain where the directions came from . . . unless . . . unless these are the same ones Jacob Waltz gave to Julia Thomas."

"We'll have to try to figure that out," Simon said. "And then maybe we'll know what happened with Uncle Hank and the gold."

Henry folded the thick piece of stationery and handed it to Delilah. "Put it in your backpack with everything else," he said. "We're going to need it."

"Okay," she said, quickly complying. "Now let me call my mom. She'll be worried about me."

"Yes, and Aunt Kathy and Emmett will be back soon. We have to clean up," Simon ordered. "Hurry!"

So Delilah quickly phoned her mother while the boys charged down the hall to the bathroom. They had never showered so quickly, one after the other, scrubbing the dust from their hair and the film of dirt from their arms and legs. The water swirling down the drain was nearly black.

"Delilah?" Henry called. "Do you want to shower too?"

She appeared in the kitchen doorway, rebraiding her hair. "No, my mom wants me to come home. I don't have clean clothes anyway. I washed off my face, and Simon gave me a brush." She hesitated. "Henry? Can I see the gold before I leave?"

"Sure! Wait here."

Jack was still in the shower when Henry opened the bathroom door and lifted his dirty pants from the tile. "Jack? Can I show Delilah the gold?"

"No!" Jack yelled, sticking his head around the shower curtain. "That's mine!"

"Oh, come on, Jack. She let us go look for the gold without her. And she warned us about the avalanche! She waited there, when she could have been smashed to smithereens by all those rocks. She saved us," he added soberly.

Jack frowned.

"Delilah's *invincible*," Henry said.

Jack sighed, water dripping down his cheeks. "Okay, you can show her," he decided. "But just this ONE TIME."

"Thanks," Henry said, fishing in Jack's pants pocket for the tiny flecks of gold. A few stuck to his fingertip, and he gently rubbed them across his palm. Under the overhead light, they glistened brilliantly.

He ducked out into the hallway and called to Delilah, his hand outstretched. "Here. You can hold them."

Delilah walked slowly toward him, eyes wide. She took the cluster of tiny gold flakes from his palm. "Look at them," she said softly. "They shine like nothing else in this world. Can you believe we found it? The Lost Dutchman's Mine?" She turned them in her palm, running her fingers lightly over them.

Henry shook his head. "I thought it might be lost forever. And now it turns out Uncle Hank beat us to it."

Delilah smiled at him, her freckled face still damp and pink from scrubbing. "Know what, Henry?"

"What?"

"I think your uncle Hank would be really proud of you. I think he'd say you're just like him."

Henry felt his heart swell, as big and light as a balloon. He grinned back at her.

"Where's my gold?" Jack yelled from the bathroom.

"Here, take it back to him." Delilah poured the gold flakes back into his hand. "I have to go anyway. See you tomorrow."

"Yeah, see you tomorrow," Henry said as she turned on her cast and clunked out the front door.

Moments later, Aunt Kathy and Emmett came bursting into the kitchen. They found the boys sitting quietly at the table, wet and glowing from their showers. Henry was so tired he imagined his bones would sink into the chair and meld there.

"Oh, my goodness!" Aunt Kathy exclaimed. "What a day we had! It was such an *adventure*, wasn't it, Emmett?"

Emmett smiled sheepishly. "Yeah, it really was. Your aunt Kathy is a good sport," he told the boys.

Aunt Kathy leaned down and kissed Henry's cheek. "You're so nice and clean," she said approvingly. "I have to tell you, you guys would have loved exploring the desert. I felt bad leaving you behind. I hope it wasn't too dull for you, spending the afternoon here by yourselves."

Henry, Simon, and Jack exchanged a small, secret glance.

"No," they said in unison.

"It was fun," Simon said.

"Yeah!" Jack echoed.

"We had adventures too," Henry added shyly.

He leaned back in the chair, and Josie promptly leapt into his lap, kneading her paws on the fabric of his pants. He stroked her soft fur, thinking of the rattlesnake and the avalanche and the gold. They had found the Lost Dutchman's Mine! The entrance was buried in rocks now, but they knew where it was. Would they be able to go back to the gold? Would they figure out how the crumpled note Josie found had been left behind in the cave, and why Uncle Hank had kept his discovery of the mine a secret? And what about the message in the dirt?

Henry thought about the strange town of Superstition, now their home. There were so many mysteries to be solved. Mrs. Thomas the librarian, who had the same name as the Julia Thomas who lived a hundred years ago— and who looked like her, and even had the same handwriting! If the old Julia Thomas from Jacob Waltz's time was buried in Phoenix, then who was in Julia Thomas's grave at the cemetery? And what about the historical society? Was it really a band of villainous treasure hunters, who would do anything to get the Lost Dutchman's gold? Anything, including murder?

Henry thought of all these things as Josie purred in his lap, content. Through the sliding door, across the shadowy yard, he could see the dark silhouette of Superstition Mountain. He knew they would be going back, despite the warning in the dirt. He wondered what surprises it held for them next.

END OF BOOK TWO

AUTHOR'S NOTE

As in book 1 of the Superstition Mountain mysteries, the town of Superstition and the contemporary characters in this novel, including the Barker boys' uncle Hank Cormody, are entirely fictitious. However, all of the historical characters and events mentioned in the story are real or based in fact. While the ghost town of Gold Creek is imaginary, it is based on actual ghost towns in the area, such as Goldfield, now a tourist attraction.

One of the more interesting historical figures is the mysterious Julia Thomas, or Julia Thomas Schaffer, a friend of the gold miner Jacob Waltz who cared for him in the months before he died. On his deathbed, Waltz purportedly gave her either a map showing the location of the Lost Dutchman's Mine or verbal directions to it. As described in *Treasure on Superstition Mountain*, in 1892, Julia Thomas went up the mountain searching for the gold in the company of German brothers Hermann and Rhinehart Petrasch. When they were unsuccessful at finding the mine, she made copies of a map that she sold to local treasure hunters for years, earning a living that way.

The map depicted in this book is based on descriptions of Julia Thomas's map, which included the detail of the "rock horse." In 1893, Julia married Albert Schaffer and moved to Phoenix, where she became involved in a religious cult, as described in the story.

The Superstition Mountain range is every bit as strange and foreboding in real life as it appears in these pages. When my daughter Zoe and I visited the area a couple of years ago, we were surprised and unsettled by how often local residents—at restaurants, gas stations, even the hotel where we were staying—warned us not to go up the mountain. "It's too dangerous," they would say. "People go missing there all the time. Hike somewhere else." But we were determined, so off we went, well supplied with water, sun lotion, and curiosity. We made the arduous hike up the Peralta Trail to Weaver's Needle, the landmark so prominent in the Barker boys' and Delilah's adventures on the mountain. The surrounding landscape was gorgeous, but harsh and isolated. It was all too easy to imagine being stranded or lost. At one point, we accidentally veered off the trail into a dry creek bed and only realized our mistake when another hiker spotted us from some distance away and yelled to us. All in all, the mountain more than lived up to its name, and in writing these mysteries, I've had no trouble channeling its spooky atmosphere . . . or its pervasive, eerie silence.

ACKNOWLEDGMENTS

IT IS A TRUE PLEASURE TO THANK the following people for their thoughtful contributions to this book:

My fabulous editor, Christy Ottaviano, who has given me the rare gift of a supportive partnership in all of my writing endeavors (not to mention a lovely friendship!). Her excellent critical eye and nimble imagination have improved my books in ways too numerous to count.

My terrific agent, Edward Necarsulmer IV, an unwavering champion of my books whose business skills make it possible for me to earn a living in this challenging field.

The excellent team at Holt, from editorial to book designers to marketing to publicity to sales, who work so hard to shepherd my books into the hands of readers.

The City of Bridgeport, Lieutenant Bob Christie and Captain Ed Martocchio of the Bridgeport Police Marine Division, and Easton

First Selectman Tom Herrmann for their kindness in arranging my private tour of a bonafide Connecticut ghost town: Pleasure Beach, an abandoned amusement park on a windswept spit of land in Bridgeport Harbor.

My writer pals, for our many discussions about plot, character, and process that have such an influence on my work: Tony Abbott, Nora Baskin, Elizabeth Bluemle, Bennett Madison, Natalie Standiford, Chris Tebbetts, Ellen Wittlinger, and Lisa Yee.

My wonderful readers, who reviewed a draft of this book under severe time pressure and whose incredibly insightful comments made it so much better: Mary Broach, Jane Burns, Claire Carlson, Laura Forte, Jane Kamensky, Carol Sheriff, Zoe Wheeler, and my younger readers, Anna Daileader Sheriff, Jane Urheim, and Margo Urheim.

Jane Kamensky and Jill Lepore, my Vermont writing retreat buddies, for all those eddies of quiet work time, dog walks, and wide-ranging conversations at Jane's house in Woodstock.

And finally, I would like to thank my amazing family—Ward, Zoe, Harry, and Grace—for, well, everything else.

ABOUT THE AUTHOR

ELISE BROACH is the author of the award-winning books *Masterpiece* and *Shakespeare's Secret*; and *Desert Crossing*. She holds undergraduate and graduate degrees in history from Yale University. She lives with her family in Easton, Connecticut.

www.elisebroach.com

ABOUT THE ILLUSTRATOR

ANTONIO JAVIER CAPARO has illustrated many books for children, including The Magic Thief series and *The Young Reader's Shakespeare: A Midsummer Night's Dream*. He lives in Montreal, Canada.

www.antoniocaparo.com